EIGHT DAYS A SURVIVOR

By Benjamin Moore

EIGHT DAYS A SURVIVOR

First edition. September 20, 2020.

Written by Benjamin Moore.

Cover art vector created with freepik - www.freepik.com https://www.freepik.com/vectors/tree

For Samma-Lamma-Ding-Dong

DAY 1

Caleb found himself alone. The sun was still up, but it was going down faster than he would have liked. He stood still, hoping to hear voices or maybe the chopping sound of an axe that someone was using to split wood to make a campfire. He heard nothing. Nothing but the soft *whoosh* of the slight breeze filtering through the tops of the pine trees. He could hear something that sounded like a creaking door hinge. Out here in the forest he knew it was the sound of trees, thick and ancient, bending slightly with the wind. Pinecones dropped from up above, producing a muffled cracking as they bounced off of lower hanging branches before landing softly in the bed of pine needles at the tree's base. Birds were chirping somewhere nearby, but none close to Caleb. Either they had fled from in front of him, not sure whether he was a threat or not, or maybe they just sat in silence, invisible to his human eyes until he moved along.

Caleb turned around, dried twigs mixed in with the pine needles crackling underfoot, and looked back in the direction from which he had just come. At least he *thought* it was the direction he came from. He tried to remember what he had learned at his scout meetings and on previous camping trips with his leaders, but his mind was not very clear. It was cooling off quickly in the shade of the trees, still sweat was staining his shirt.

Should I keep moving? Should I go back where I came from? Should I stay still? He didn't know and the unknowing made his heart race. He was scared. Caleb closed his eyes to keep himself calm. He tried to ease his breathing by taking deep breaths. He opened his eyes again to look around one more time, hoping with all his might that he would see something to help him make his decision.

Turning back to his left he caught sight of the sun. It was no longer the bright, burning white globe directly overhead. It was now a muted orange ball whose bottom edge was just now touching the mountainous horizon. Though he was rattled and scared, he was able to pull himself together enough to know that he was losing daylight. He needed to figure out where he was going to sleep before it truly got dark. His wanderings were over for the day and it was time to accept that he would be by himself for the night. His hopes of being quickly found after being separated from the rest of his troop of scouts were dashed.

Caleb was truly alone for the first time in his life and he was scared.

•••••

Holman lifted his head, opened his eyes, and rose from his knees. He had been praying with all earnestness for guidance on what he should do. Caleb had been missing for over six hours. Holman, along with the other camp leaders, was still clueless as to where the boy was. So many thoughts were racing through his head: *How did he get separated from the group? Where was the last time anyone saw him? Would he stay still or keep moving?* And then the dreaded questions: *What if we can't find him? What do I tell his parents? How do I face them?*

"Holman?" came a questioning voice from behind him. Holman turned and saw the two other scout leaders. It was Jaylen who had addressed him. Jaylen was the official leader of the trip, but now that a crisis had emerged, they all, the leaders and the boys, looked to Holman. Leadership is something that can be taught and learned, yet there are some people in life that just have it naturally. He was one of those people.

"Jaylen, Alex", he acknowledged the men, nodding his head at each as he said their names.

"What do you think?" asked Jaylen. "It's getting late and the other boys are tired and scared. Alex and I think it would probably be a good idea to make camp and make the biggest fire we can, without setting the whole forest ablaze. Then maybe, after we eat, we can go out in teams for a little while longer looking for Caleb." Holman contemplated his words for a moment, and then nodded his head. The big fire was a good idea. If Caleb was anywhere nearby he might see the light and be able to make his way back to them.

"That's probably best. Why don't you two follow through on that, I'll go out and look for a little bit longer, before it's completely dark." Holman brought his wrist up and pressed a button on his watch. "I've marked this location's GPS coordinates on my watch, so I know exactly how to get back to you if I too lose my way." He paused to sip water from his bottle. He then pulled his flashlight out of a cargo pocket on his pants and turned it on, pointing it at the palm of his hand to check the batteries. After verifying it was working well, he switched it off and pocketed it. "All right, I'm off. I won't be gone long. I'll try and be back not long after dusk", he said to Alex and Jaylen and they nodded in response. With that he turned and disappeared into the forest.

• • • • •

Caleb had laid his sleeping bag down on the ground and was now curled up inside of it. There was a thin layer of needles beneath him, only not enough to cushion his body from the hard earth underneath. He had an inflatable sleeping pad in his pack, yet he didn't get it out. Being mentally and physically exhausted from the day, he just wanted to lay down. He hadn't eaten or drunk any water in at least a couple of hours and, unknown to him, it was affecting his ability to make good decisions. Of course, he knew hydrating was important. He didn't realize, though, that with all his hiking and yelling for help and sweating that he had used up a lot more of his body's water reserves than he would have thought. Playing video games back at home didn't really prepare him to be mindful about hydration. With his water levels getting low, his brain's ability to think clearly was becoming more blurred.

Throughout the night he tossed and turned, unable to get comfortable enough to fall asleep. Even if he had been comfortable, he more than likely would not have slept. His mind was racing and the darkness that surrounded him caused each small sound to become sinister and frightening.

At one point in the evening he thought he heard the faintest sound of his name being called. His heart burst through his chest and he exploded from his sleeping bag, breaking the zipper in the process. He turned on his flashlight and spun around, pointing it in all directions.

"I'm over here!!" he screamed as loud as his small lungs would allow, waving his arms over his head, as if someone could see him in the dark. "OVER HERE!! I'm over here!" he yelled. Pausing to listen, all he could hear was the pounding of his own heartbeat in his ears. "Please! Help me! I'm over here!" came out a yell that was transformed into sobs. He dropped onto his knees on the forest floor. "Please! Please", he cried, "I'm lost...I'm so scared." He fell down to his side, curled up into a ball, and cried his heart out. He had held himself together rather well for the whole day, now he was finally letting himself be scared. The release of all of the emotions that he had kept at bay flowed out onto dried pine needles in the form of tears.

•••••

Holman paused mid-stride, his ears perking up. He was making his way back to the camp and was yelling Caleb's name in all directions. He was not far from the campsite, less than half a mile, and was still searching. After one of his yells he thought that he heard a reply. He couldn't be sure, as he was yearning to hear a response; sometimes the nighttime plays tricks not only on your sight, but on your hearing as well. He stood still, trying to breathe as quietly as possible. Nothing. He turned his head in the direction he thought the voice had come from and yelled again. Still no reply.

"Must be my ears playing tricks on me," he said under his breath, barely audible even to himself. After that episode, he stopped raising his voice and made off in the direction of the rest of the campers. Little did he know that a quarter of a mile away, and less than a mile from the group, young Caleb had just burst out of his sleeping bag and was frantically yelling. It was the closest thing to human contact that the young boy would have for quite some time.

DAY 2

Caleb woke the next morning with the sun already above what would be the horizon, if he could have seen it through the trees. He was bundled up in his cushy sleeping bag, nevertheless he was freezing. He had eventually found sleep, though it was not very restful. His mind had raced all night. When he did get it to calm down enough, he still shivered uncontrollably. In reality, it wasn't all that cold this time of year, but the slight chill, combined with the shock of being lost, resulted in a feeling of coldness all through his bones.

He sat up in the bag, his left shoulder exposed as the zipper would no longer go up all the way after breaking it the night before. He looked around. There was nothing around him that he recognized, it was all just forest. He pulled his hands from inside the bag and rubbed his eyes. Instead of giving him relief, the action hurt because his eyes were so dry. He tried swallowing and that also pained him. He slid the rest of the way out of the sleeping bag and retrieved his 32oz. water bottle that was clipped on the outside of his backpack with a carabiner. A carabiner is a special clip normally used for rock climbing, but works perfect for so many other things camping related. He drank half a bottle's worth of water...nothing had ever tasted better.

After downing his drink, his stomach began to rumble and hurt immensely. He opened another pocket on the backpack and pulled out some beef jerky. He sat with his back up against a pine tree and slowly ate several pieces. It was his favorite-- teriyaki flavored. His mom bought it for him for all his camping trips because she knew that he loved it.

While he sat there, he was able to think about his situation. The water and food in his body were slowly giving him back an improved ability to think clearly. Having made it through the dark night, he had calmed down drastically compared to before getting some rest. He began to speak out loud, he often did so in order to more effectively organize his thoughts.

"I'm lost. Mr. Holman and everyone is probably looking for me. I should have stayed in the same spot I was in once I realized I was lost, but it's too late for that now. So, should I keep moving or should I stay here?" He looked around more critically at his surroundings. "I could stay here; there's plenty of wood on the ground for me to make a fire. I could also make some sort of shelter out of the branches on the trees," he said as he put another piece of jerky in his mouth. After swallowing, he took a swig of water from his bottle and his eyes lingered on the remaining water.

"Crap." Caleb realized two things at the same moment. First, there was wood on the ground that looked dried out enough to burn, but he had no way of lighting a fire. No matches, no lighter, no fire starter. Second, he would need a water source and there wasn't one that he could see or hear from where he sat. He focused on trying to remember what his scouting troop leaders had taught him about food and water. *How long can a human go without food and water? 30 days without water?*

"No," he said, "too long, I think it's 30 days without food. Or is it three weeks?" He remembered that there was a "Rule of Threes" for surviving. Like most kids in his troop, he paid enough attention to earn his rank and achievement patches, but didn't retain as much knowledge as the leaders would have liked. He was a scout because it was fun to be with his friends and to go on adventures and campouts.

"Caleb," he said to himself, "this is an adventure. This is an *adventure*. Now think!" He tried to remember for sure, but couldn't be certain. "Well, I know water is more important than food, and if I can make it three weeks without food, then maybe I can do no water for three days." He thought about how dry his eyes and throat and mouth were after just one night of not drinking enough. "Yeah, three days. That's gotta be it."

With that resolved, he realized that his current location would not be a good place to set up. He needed to get into 'survival mode'. He didn't know how long he would be out here alone, but the situation called for him to get in the mindset that he would be out here for a while.

Caleb didn't have a map or a compass with him. If he had had those items, he might have been able to figure out where he was, and where he needed to go. He got up, closed the resealable teriyaki beef jerky bag, and put it back into his pack. He slid the top of the jerky bag, which he had ripped off to open it, into his backpack as well. It was a force of habit that caused him to put his trash into the pocket he had retrieved it from. One of the 'golden rules' of being outdoors is 'Pack It In, Pack It Out'. In other words: don't leave a trail of trash. In this instance though, he also thought, *I might be able to use this for something in the future.* Going to the store and picking up more food or supplies was obviously not an option; Caleb had with him what he had. He knew he had to treat everything like a survival tool that could assist him, though he had no idea how a small piece of plastic might help.

He rolled up his sleeping bag and tied it, then put it in the large compartment of his backpack. With that done, he slung the pack onto his back, buckled the waist belt, and looked around. He tried to decide which course he ought to take in his quest for water. He looked towards the rising sun, knowing that heading in that direction would be roughly east. Unfortunately, that didn't help him figure out where the closest water source might be, nor did it aid him in knowing which route offered the best chance of finding help. In the end, he decided to 'head towards the light' and set off eastward.

His heart started beating fast again and he became nervous. It's amazing how quickly a human being can become familiar with and attached to a location. Just the night before Caleb had never set foot in this place. Now, when he was about to leave it, he was hesitant to do so. It already felt more 'safe' than the unknown. "It's an adventure," he said under his breath and took the first step away from his campsite.

•••••

That same morning some of the boys rose early and gathered around the remains of the previous night's bonfire. They were all quiet, staring into the still hot charcoals of the fire, hands stuffed into their pockets. The leaders were off to the side of where the boys had clustered and were discussing their options.

"Here are my thoughts," Holman started out, "I'd love to be able to go back out and keep searching. I feel like if we don't search ourselves then we are sacrificing time and possibly distance from Caleb. We don't know if he's staying put or out there moving around. I also feel an immense responsibility for him being out there all alone, I just couldn't sleep at all last night. I'm so torn up about it."

"Me too", Jaylen said, and Alex nodded along in silence.

"That being said, if he's not staying put, we might just be running circles around each other. I think the right choice is for us to get professional help. We need search and rescue that has access to helicopters and all that stuff. We also need to get the other boys back to safety before they, or one of us, gets into an additional predicament." Holman looked over to where the scouts had gathered around the fire ring, then continued, "We need to notify his family as well. It has only been one night, but it's their right to know about their boy. If it were my son, I'd want to know." After that last comment they sat around for a couple more minutes. Holman rose and said, "Let's rouse the boys that are still sleeping and get a move on, we don't want to waste any more time."

With that Jaylen and Alex got up and gently woke the scouts still laying in their sleeping bags and told them to pack up. Holman asked the boys to use the shovel to cover the campfire with dirt to extinguish it completely. Instead of the hot oatmeal they were planning on having, they would have granola and energy bars with water as they hiked out.

Alex approached Holman, "We need to get the boys back to the trucks and get them home. However, for the sake of time, I think it might be a good idea if I run ahead to the parking lot and drive my truck until I get a cell signal or run into a ranger." Alex, despite being the quiet leader of the group, was someone that the scouts were in awe of. Mr. Alex, as they called him, was an ultra-marathoner. He considered a 10 mile trail run a warm up. He had even run the famous Grand Canyon Rim-to-Rim-to-Rim trail several times, taking him from the South Rim, down to the Colorado River, up to the North Rim, and then all the way back in one day. He would be able to get back to the trucks they had driven to the trailhead hours before the boys would arrive.

After some thought Holman said, "Go for it, Alex, be safe." Alex nodded, chugged some water from one of his bottles, kept one small full bottle, and distributed the rest to the scouts, lightening his load. He cinched his pack tightly to his back and adjusted his chest strap. He looked at the boys.

"Boys, we are going to do everything that we can to find Caleb. I'll be honest, we can't guarantee anything beyond that. He might be just fine, he could be hurt, we don't know. Just know that we'll use every resource available to find him, and we'll do it as fast as we can, so we can bring him back home." With that he gave a final look at the other leaders, nodded his head in a mild salute, then turned and took off down the trail.

•••••

Caleb had been walking for, what felt to him, like a couple of hours. His legs were sore as today was the fourth day in a row that he had been hiking *and* he was carrying a pack, though it wasn't very heavy if he was being honest about it. He stopped in a small clearing where a tree had been uprooted and had fallen over. Looking at the timber, he thought about what might have led to its fall, and then wondered what a loud sound it must have made when it hit the ground. It probably made quite a racket and caused all the birds nearby to take flight, screeching cries of warning to all within earshot. He sat on the downed tree's large trunk after he had removed and leaned his pack up against it. Taking out his bottle Caleb took stock of what still remained of his water. He was tempted to save it for when he was extremely thirsty, but then he remembered some of the stories he had heard.

Apparently there had been people in the past that had been lost or stranded and, when they were eventually located, were found dead. The *crazy* thing is that they still had water in their bottles or canteens! Caleb and the boys couldn't believe it. The stories pointed out that rescuers believed that the people that had been found tried to save their water, to make it last longer. In the end, they got so dehydrated that they stopped making good decisions and wound up dying of thirst...while they still had water. Caleb looked at the little water he had and, although his instincts were telling him to conserve it, he removed the cap and downed it all. "Better to store it in my body than in a bottle," he remarked, and he replaced the top of the bottle and then the bottle in his bag.

With that over and done with he said out loud, "Now I *really* need to find a water source." He took out his baggie of trail mix and looked at it. He intended to eat some of the snack, but paused when he opened it up. He contemplated whether it would be a wiser choice to save the food for later. He decided to have a handful and then put the baggie back in his backpack before he caved in to his hunger and ate more than that. He popped a small amount into his mouth. Nothing in his life had ever tasted better than those salty peanuts mixed with the sweet raisins and M&M's. He savored the flavor for a full minute, letting the chewed up mixture just sit on his tongue before swallowing. The joy derived from the food was short lived, though, as he quickly returned to the dire reality in which he now found himself. Water. He needed water.

He stood up on the log to have a look around. He couldn't see very far because of the trees, but he did see the top of a small hill. He remembered that water, whether rainwater or melting snow, is always pulled downhill due to gravity. Caleb thought that if he headed towards that hill there might be some water at the base of it that he could fill his bottle with. He wasn't sure if that would work, but it was better than wandering aimlessly.

While still energized from the water and the trail mix he just ate, he once again slipped his arms through the straps of the hiking pack, starting off in the direction of the hill.

•••••

Alex arrived back at the trucks a little bit before

noon. Despite being in great shape and an experienced trail runner, he wasn't used to running with a large pack full of camping gear. He had given out some of his items to lighten the load, even so it was still bulky and heavy. He was exhausted because of that, but also partially because he had really pushed himself. He wasn't out for a training run or to just get out into the beauty of nature, he had been running to possibly save a boy's life. So, he ran hard and made it back to the parking lot faster than even he had thought possible.

He threw his pack into the bed of his full sized, silver Ford pickup truck and filled his water bottle from the big water container that had been left in the back of Holman's truck, a white Chevy with a bed cover on it. He chugged it all in one go and refilled it again immediately. With that done, he set the now full bottle on the edge of his truck bed and laid down in the dirt near his left rear tire. He crawled under the vehicle, located and removed a hidden magnetic box, and took a spare key out of it. He had attached the small box to the frame in case he ever lost his keys. He hadn't forgotten them or misplaced them, he had just decided to use the spare on this trip so that he wouldn't have to carry his key ring on the campout.

Alex unlocked the vehicle and slid onto the shiny, worn leather bench seat. There were cracks in the material, mostly on the driver's side, and one could see some of the material and stuffing inside. He had been planning on getting the seat redone, but just hadn't gotten around to it yet.

He plugged a cell phone charging cord into a power converter and inserted the other end of the cord into the bottom of the cell phone. The screen lit up when it started charging. At the top of the display there was an indicator showing 13% battery life remaining with a flashing lightning bolt next to it, indicating that it was charging. What *wasn't* there was the symbol signifying that the phone was connected to a network. He knew there would be no signal, yet he had still hoped against hope anyway. You never know, there might have been some sort of cosmic radio wave superstorm somewhere out there that would boost his signal. No luck.

Alex pressed the power button on the side of the phone and the screen went dark. He then set the phone in the holder that was attached to the dashboard. He inserted the truck key and turned it, starting the engine with a deep rumble. It was an ugly, old truck, but the engine and transmission still ran great. The vehicle was his 'adventure truck'; looks didn't matter, only performance. He dropped the car into gear and peeled out from the lot, leaving behind a huge cloud of dust to settle on the other vehicles.

He drove for an hour before getting a weak signal indication on the phone. He tried calling for help a few times, but he kept getting disconnected. When the signal symbol on the display was consistently strong, he pulled over again. To his frustration, he had to drive for another half an hour before being able to get through without dropping the call.

"Forest Service, this is Ranger Smargiassi", said the voice on the other end of the line.

"Hello, Ranger Smarg..., uh, sir, my name is Alex Milner. I was out in the backcountry with a group of scouts. We started at the trailhead just north of milepost 39 and one of the boys got separated from the group yesterday. We spread out, backtracked, and looked for him, but still haven't located him," he said out of breath.

"When exactly was the boy last seen?" the ranger asked. Alex could hear a faint scratching sound, what he imagined was the scribbling of pen on paper, in the background of the call. The man was writing all this down. Alex gave him all the information he could about time, location, what Caleb looked like, what he was wearing, and what supplies he may have had with him. Alex was put on hold as the man contacted his supervisor over the radio. When he came back on the line the ranger informed him that the supervisor would be contacting the search and rescue team.

"Will they send out a helicopter? I guess you probably don't know that. I'll have to ask the search and rescue guys," Alex said.

"Well, I happen to know that the helo is not in the local area right now, but will be back by tomorrow morning. Don't get your heart set on that being the make or break part of this search, though. Helicopters are a fantastic tool and are very handy, especially when extracting an injured person. Still, don't underestimate the value of boots on the ground during a search," the ranger advised.

"You're right," Alex said, "you guys know better than us and have the right tools. I guess that's why I contacted you as soon as I could." He paused again to catch his breath and think about his next move. "Well, I've passed on all the info I have. I'm going to drive back and make sure that the rest of the group got back safe and we can get the other boys back home to their families."

"That's probably a good idea," the ranger said. "I'm Ted by the way. My lady friend, Tawna, she's the local search and rescue coordinator, that's how I know what's going on with the helicopter that they use."

"Nice to meet you Ted, I wish it wasn't under these particular circumstances, though."

"Agreed," said Ted. "Well, why don't you go ahead and return to your group of scouts. You'll be out of cell coverage again, but we've already covered the essential points. Just make sure when you send the boys on their way that you, or at least one of the other leaders, stay behind as a point of contact for Tawna and the search and rescue team. I'm sure that they will have additional questions and will need one of you along to provide possible insight."

"Ok, will do." Alex didn't know what else to say, so he signed off with the standard, "I'll see you later", even though he wasn't sure there would be any "seeing" of the ranger.

"Take care, Alex," Ted came back, "keep the faith. The boy hasn't been gone long and the weather is agreeable." Alex nodded his head and tapped the screen on his phone to hang up the call. With that, he turned on his left blinker, looked over his shoulder to see if there were any other cars coming down the highway, and then pulled out into the road and made a U-turn, heading back to the trailhead.

•••••

Caleb had been making his way in the direction of the hill for hours now, but it was just now finally appearing to be closer. For the majority of his time hiking towards the hill it looked like it was forever going to be off in the far distance. Now, he was practically upon it.

Not long after this observation, he arrived at what might be considered the base of the hill. There was nothing distinct about the terrain, other than a slight incline. What made him feel like he had reached this distinctive point was the fact that there was a feeble trickle of water on the ground in front of him. The water flowed in a low, mostly dry riverbed that Caleb could tell was a large river when it was raining or when snow was melting. The small trickle of water cut through the far side of the riverbed, moving from his left to right.

He felt thirsty after having hiked for so long without hydration. Now that he saw and —maybe even more enticing— heard the light gurgling of the water he rushed towards it, dropping down to his hands and knees. As he fell forward, the center of gravity of his pack moved over his head and the frame crashed into the back of his head, causing him to face plant in dirt. He sat back up and had he had a mirror he would have seen his chin, cheeks, and nose covered in sand and pine needles. He laughed at himself after landing on his face as he looked at the moving water.

Caleb recovered himself and steadied his body on his left elbow as he used his right hand to scoop water up to his mouth. The water wasn't very deep, but he got as much as he could while minimizing the dirt in his mouth. After he had satisfied his thirst he stood up and wiped the mess from his face, palms, and the knees of his pants. Then he started off in the direction of the flowing water.

As he hiked, his mind began to wander, as it had for most of the day. He had thought about many things. Mostly he had been trying to figure out where he had gone wrong. How had he gotten separated from his troop? The first two days and nights they had all been together and there had been no issues. The boys had practiced building shelters, tying knots, making fire, orienteering, and a few other tasks. They were all working towards some sort of badge or rank advancement and were putting in the work, though it mostly didn't feel like working. They had also done plenty of goofing around, of course. After all, they were a bunch of young boys with energy to burn.

The leaders allowed the scouts to be loud and crazy, as long as it wasn't during one of their instructional periods. That was one of the best things about being out in the woods! Rules that applied at home didn't apply when you were camping. Use a napkin to clean your hands during a meal? No way; the boys wiped their dirty hands on their pants. Runny noses need tissue or a handkerchief, right? Forget about it; snot was wiped off faces with shirtsleeves in the chilly mornings. Burps or farts at the dinner table would get you sent to the laundry room to finish your meal standing up and your plate on the washer. But camping? Farting and burping was not only allowed around camp, but was encouraged by all! Both of which often turned into some sort of contest. Voices which were constantly being described as "too loud" inside their homes were perfectly acceptable out here; yelling was the normal form of communication. Running was standard, rough housing was expected, and throwing anything you could find into the fire was completely cool—as long as it wasn't plastic or Styrofoam. Caleb and the rest of the boys LOVED camping and being in the outdoors.

Unfortunately, not everyone appreciated the noise and craziness of the scouts. Not all of their camping trips were backpacking in the back country, like they were on this trip, where they didn't see anyone else the whole time. Sometimes they camped in a campground with others around. While the boys were told by their leaders to keep it down after dark, they were still pretty crazy up until that point. One time, one of the people they were sharing a campground with came up to Caleb's dad—who was one of the leaders on that particular trip—and asked, "Can you tell your boys to be quiet and respect the other campers?" Caleb's dad got red in the face and told the person, respectfully, that they came to the outdoors so that they didn't have to keep their voices down. Once it got dark, they would tell them to quiet down, but until then they would just have to be okay with the noise. The other camper walked away very unhappy and the boys that witnessed the exchange struggled to hide their laughter.

Later that same night, as they all sat around the campfire making s'mores, an old beat up van with a mural of, what they assumed to be, the family's favorite football team pulled into the last remaining spot...right next to the person that complained about the noise. The doors to the van swung open and out poured a family of eight, none of the kids older than 10 years old, and the youngsters immediately dispersed into the surrounding woods. They were hooting and hollering, throwing things at each other, and breaking down half the forest from the sound of it all. The pure joy on his father's face was something Caleb would never forget. The flickering orange glow of the fire danced across his insuppressible smile as he sipped hot chocolate from his camping cup.

Caleb smiled as he recalled this memory, then he came back to his original question: How did this happen? He remembered having breakfast with everyone else and then cleaning up their campsite. The boys wanted to play more games, but the leaders said that they should get moving to the next campsite. Once there, and after they had set everything up, they'd have plenty of time to explore and horse around some more. They packed up their individual items, washed out mess kits and spoons used for their breakfast of oatmeal, and walked around the camp making sure no trash was being left behind.

Some of the boys were ready to head out long before the others and asked Mr. Holman if they could start moving. Holman said he would go with them, but that they'd have to take it easy so the others could catch up without having to rush. Caleb was almost ready and wanted to go with them. Upon seeing them leaving he hurried to wash the oatmeal out of his camping bowl and to wipe off his spoon. Once that was put away and his sleeping pad and bag were stowed properly, he sat down to retie his hiking boots. After tightening the laces, he lifted his pack and called over his shoulder to Mr. Jaylen and Mr. Alex that he was going to chase down the group that had already left.

He had hiked fast, staying on the clearly worn path. So, where had they gone? He just couldn't figure out why he hadn't been able to find them. Unfortunately for Caleb, what he didn't know was that less than 100 yards down the path there had been a fork in the trail. There was a trail marker naming each of the trails, but Caleb was hiking fast and had his head down. He didn't see the marker, nor did he notice that there had been a fork in the path. He headed off on what he thought was the only trail, but in reality it was the route that the other boys had not taken.

It was now many hours since he had started hiking and the sun was going down. He was so relieved to have found water that he felt that he could handle anything, darkness falling was nothing. His number one priority had been taken care of. He hiked a little bit further and decided that there was no need to rush now that he had achieved his immediate goal. Caleb removed his pack, set it flat on the ground by the base of a tree, and sat down on top of it and leaned back.

Caleb awoke about an hour later and noticed the sun was already fully down. He didn't mean to, but as soon as he had leaned his head back against the large tree trunk, he had closed his eyes and immediately fell asleep. By the time he woke up it was too late to make a shelter. He took out his flashlight and used it to find a mostly level spot on the ground with no rocks or roots to contend with. Once he had located the spot he turned off the light and worked in the pale dusk, he was trying to conserve as much battery power in his flashlight as he could.

He dragged his pack over to his sleeping area, took out his sleeping bag, and removed his sleeping pad. He blew up the pad and laid the bag down on top of it. Once that was set up—it didn't take long—he grabbed his water bottle and knelt down by the small stream. At this point the flow wasn't even enough to warrant the title of 'stream', but he didn't know what else to call it, so that's what it was.

He laid the bottle down on its side in the water and let it fill as much as it would, then picked it back up. He tilted his head back and opened his mouth wide, raising the bottle up. He went to take a big gulp of water, unfortunately what he got was a mouth full of soggy dirt, pebbles, and some pine needles. He spat the nasty mixture onto the ground in front of him and tried to wipe his tongue off with the sleeve of his jacket. This was not going to do at all.

Caleb thought about what to do. The water wasn't deep enough to just put the bottle in the stream and get water free of debris; a filter of some sort was needed. He wasn't worried about filtering the water for bacteria since it was moving. He had been taught that moving water was fresh and usually safe, but stagnant or puddled water was bad. The problem was just getting the water so that he could drink it, not chew it. After a few moments he thought he might have come up with the solution.

He went back to his pack and dug down in the bottom. After a moment, his hand emerged with a blue hiking sock...one that was not clean. He rolled up his nose at the smell, but took it back over to the stream anyway. He laid it gently in the water trying to not grind any mud into it and to just let it soak. Once thoroughly wet, he picked it up and wrung it out tightly. He repeated this sequence two more times and then thought it was enough.

Well, that's probably as good as it's going to get, he thought.

After the final wringing out, he pulled the socked over the mouth of the container and laid it back down in the water. He was hoping that the sock was porous enough to allow water to seep through it, but not so porous as to permit other debris into the bottle. After a minute he lifted the container out of the flowing water and removed the sock. He turned on his flashlight for a moment and shined it into the bottle. The water looked all right. A few grains of sand had made it through the sock filter, but other than that it seemed to have done the trick. He switched off the light and drank the contents of the container, enjoying every cool, fresh drop.

Caleb ate handfuls of trail mix while he repeated the process a few more times with the sock filter. The final time he filled the bottle he left the water inside, removed the sock, and screwed the cap on. He would set the container next to his sleeping bag in case he wanted a drink in the night.

With water and a small amount of food in his belly, he pulled on his winter hat and slipped into his sleeping bag. Before he closed his eyes he stared up at the starry night. The lack of a bright moon and city lights made it so he could see, what he imagined were, billions of stars. He knew that some of the "stars" he was seeing were actually galaxies that were far enough away to appear to the naked eye as a single star. That was something he was taught at a week-long astronomy camp he had attended last summer. He had learned so much about stars, planets, galaxies, and nebulas. It was the coolest camp he ever went to and he couldn't wait to go again.

After a few moments he came back to the reality of his current situation. He needed to be found or to find someone in order to go to the astronomy camp again, or any camp for that matter. He stared up into the vastness of the celestial heavens and, eyes still open, said aloud in a pleading voice, "Please, please help them to find me. Please help me."

DAY 3

Alex had returned to the parking lot after contacting the Rangers the previous evening, arriving around the same time that the other scouts and leaders showed up. The boys were tired, dirty, and scared for their friend. He could see, as they shuffled past the trailhead marker into the lot, that a few of the scouts had streaks of tears marking clear paths down through the dust on their cheeks.

After the boys, as well as the leaders, had gotten what rest they could manage for the rest of the night, Holman was trying to figure out how to get everyone where they needed to be. They wouldn't be able to fit all the boys into one vehicle, so only one of the leaders could stay behind as they needed two to drive. Alex had been the point of contact with the Ranger, but one of the scouts in the group was his own son, so it was determined he ought to be one of the drivers. Holman offered to stay and wait for the search and rescue team and Jaylen agreed and said he would drive the other truck.

Before the boys climbed into the cabs of the trucks, and after having already eaten a small breakfast, they tossed their camping gear into the truck beds in a loose pile and gathered around Holman. They were all completely exhausted and each one seemed to be staring off into space, focusing on some unseen object. Though some wouldn't have openly admitted it, they were ready to go home and shower and cry and be held by their parents, but they were also hesitant to leave. Their friend was still out there somewhere and, although they didn't quite know what it was, it felt like they were abandoning him forever. They were scared that the finality of their leaving would somehow influence his survival.

Holman noticed their hesitation and asked them to gather around. Standing together they each put their arms around their neighbor's shoulders, forming a tight circle. The emotion of the moment was instantaneously intense, a couple of the boys were trying to keep themselves from openly weeping.

"We are going to do everything humanly possible to find Caleb. The Ranger told Mr. Alex that the weather is good, it doesn't look like it is going to be raining anytime soon, and it's not getting too cold at night. Caleb won't have to battle the elements to try and stay warm and dry. That is a really big thing and it swings in his favor," Holman said. Some of the boys took in his words while staring down at their feet, others kept their chins up.

"Another thing to remember, we've all been trained for outdoor survival, Caleb included. We know that you boys don't retain everything that we teach you, but the core principles we have taught are there inside all of you," he continued, pointing around the small circle of bodies. "He will remember what we've all learned and keep himself alive and safe long enough for us to find him. He's smart, like all of you."

"But he's alone," came a meek voice from one of the young scouts.

"He is, Kevin, but he knows we're going to be looking for him. He knows he is loved. He has all the tools we've given him on previous camping trips to help him out. He'll be so busy surviving that, hopefully, he doesn't have too much time to worry about being alone." Holman paused and finally said, "We're going to find him, we're gonna do it."

Before they broke the circle another of the boys asked, "Can we say a prayer for him?" Not all of the boys in the group went to the same church and a couple didn't even go to church. In the moment, though, they all felt that asking for any sort of help that might be out there was a good idea.

"Of course we can, David. Would you like to say it?" Holman asked. The boy nodded and proceeded to give a short, heartfelt, very sincere prayer asking that Caleb be watched over and kept safe. He concluded the prayer by pleading that Caleb would be found soon and unharmed. When the prayer was finished the boys stayed in their tight circle for a few moments and then they slowly broke the circle, gradually making their way into the waiting vehicles.

Holman could see, and eventually hear, the arrival of a small caravan of vehicles as the group separated. The assortment of automobiles, mostly trucks set up for off road driving, pulled up next to his tent in the parking area. The group of vehicles brought with them a large cloud of dust that caused Holman to close his eyes and cover his mouth and nose with a bandana. After the dust settled, Holman looked up at the sound of slamming car doors and saw the silhouettes of people walking up to him. A woman came forward and offered her hand.

"Hello, I'm Tawna." Holman took the hand and shook it. Once she had stepped closer to him, and into better light, he saw that she was a shorter woman with large, thick-framed glasses perched on her nose. She had earrings that were in the lobes of her ears that had holes in the centers large enough to fit a dime through. He could also see the edge of a tattoo peeking out from underneath her collar. She was wearing a jacket now and he couldn't see them, but he would've bet money on her having more tattoos covering her arms as well.

"Hi, I'm Holman."

"Nice to meet you. Ted said that there's a young boy out there that got separated from your troop?"

"Yes, tonight is the second night he's been out on his own. His name is Caleb."

"Okay, let's go over all the information that was given to Ted. I'll ask you some additional questions and we'll figure out a good plan of attack," Tawna said and led Holman over to the truck she had just gotten out of. She had the rest of her search team introduce themselves to Holman while she laid out a map of the area onto the hood of the vehicle. After the introductions, Tawna handed Holman a highlighter pen and said, "Please, highlight the path you and the rest of your group took from beginning to end."

Holman complied and, after doing so, used the pen to circle the second night's campsite. While tapping the spot with the bottom of the pen, he said, "Right here is the last time we saw Caleb. We saw him leave camp with all his gear and we haven't seen him since. He was trying to catch up to some of the boys that had left just a few minutes before him." After a pause he continued, "We, another leader and I that were back with the slower boys, caught up to the group that left earlier and we were surprised to find that Caleb wasn't with them. We all stopped and a couple of us went back to look for him. Obviously, we didn't find him."

Tawna and another member of the group, leaning over her shoulder, contemplated the map closely. They were pointing out some areas with a pen and discussing some of the other trails in the area and the terrain. After a few moments they had a plan.

"We're going to take the quads off the back of the trucks," she said turning and indicating the small off-road vehicles high up on some of the truck beds, "and get out to the campsite. He might have made his way back there and is waiting for help. If not, we'll spread out, following some of these other nearby trails. He might hear the engines and hopefully we find him quick."

"And if not?" Holman asked.

"Well, we've got other things we can do, but let's concentrate on that for now and we can cross that bridge when we get to it."

With that, the quads were unloaded, first aid and rescue gear was tightened down on their racks, and radio batteries were checked. After that, the team members buzzed off into the forest. A few minutes later they were no more to be seen or heard by Holman or Tawna. She had stayed behind as she was the search commander and this parking lot was now home base.

•••••

When Caleb awoke his nose felt completely frozen; it felt like an icicle. He was bundled up in his sleeping bag, but in the night he had needed to keep pulling the top flap of the bag over his face because of the broken zipper. It was long before the cold season, still it got quite chilly out in the wild.

He sat up in the bag and contemplated getting up. His body was achy and he did not feel like doing anything. He felt like it was Saturday morning back at home and his mom was waking him up before 10:00...he just didn't want to do it.

The thought of his mom woke him fully. He missed her and he knew that he needed to get moving if he was going to get back to her. He pulled the sleeping bag flap away from his shoulder and stood up, grabbing his water bottle from the earth as he did so. He had drunk the little bit that was in the container during the night and it was now empty. He slipped his feet into his boots without tying them and shuffled lazily to a tree not far away where he unzipped his pants to relieve himself. He hadn't peed in a long time and it was a good sign that he needed to now; he was starting to get enough water back into his system and was staying hydrated.

He zipped the front of his pants back up and moved over to the stream to fill his bottle. He had just finished slipping the sock back over the container's opening and was stooping down at the water's edge when he saw something that stopped his heart. In the damp earth next to the small stream was a large paw print. He couldn't remember clearly whether it had been there the night before or not and the hairs on the back of his neck and arms stood on end. His scalp began tingling and he felt his ears become hot. He shot to his feet and spun around several times, trying to look in all directions at once. He felt very exposed and vulnerable.

Up until now, Caleb had been so focused on finding water and surviving the elements that he hadn't really thought about there being animals out in the forest that might see him as a nice meal. His heart beat so fast he thought he was having a panic attack; he was having real trouble controlling his breathing. His hands started shaking and he closed his eyes and spoke to himself, "Calm down, Caleb, calm down." He concentrated on his breathing and took slow, deep breaths through his nose while trying to calm his mind.

When he opened his eyes again, he knelt down next to the paw print and looked at it more closely. He stretched out his fingers and compared the size of his hand to that of the print. From the size of it and taking note of the long claw marks he thought it might be from a bear, something he knew lived in these woods. Again, he wasn't sure whether it was there last night or not, but it looked like there was a mild depression on one edge of the print. He came to the conclusion that the indentation was from his knee when he had knelt and filled his bottle, which would mean that it was there before he had arrived at the spot. He exhaled a breath in relief, evidently a bear *hadn't* come through his campground last night.

The relief was short-lived though. Yes, the paw print was made before he arrived, but there was wildlife out there with him. Wildlife that could rip him apart with ease. Another thought crossed his mind: the paw print was right next to the stream and he realized that there were other animals out here that were also interested in the same water source as him. For all he knew, he was in an area that was another animal's territory, he did *not* want to be caught "trespassing". Tonight, if he was still out here, he would try to find a place to camp that wasn't so close to the water.

By midday Caleb had followed the water for what he thought was several miles. He kept thinking about animals coming to the water and this worried him. He also thought that if animals were attracted to water then, hopefully, humans would be too. He was torn between staying in one place or continuing to move. The paw print had freaked him out, but he decided to stay close to the stream. He hoped to run into his scout group or some other campers along the flowing water.

The stream, while still not a large body of moving water at all, had widened and deepened in most places along his route, so much so that he could now submerge his bottle fully. He thought he could now do without the sock filter, but used it anyway. After filling up and replacing the bottle cap, he leaned back down at the water's edge and splashed water on his face. He had started feeling the crustiness of the dirt that had gathered there, and it felt good to wash it off.

He retreated from the water and sat down to rest his swollen feet. Finding a good spot to sit and lean against a tree, he removed his boots to air out his socks and feet. He opened up the second small bag of beef jerky that he had brought with him and ate the last two pieces. He had eaten some this morning not long after he left his campsite. He looked into his backpack compartment at what remained of his food. There were a couple of instant oatmeal packets and a bag of trail mix. He was terribly hungry, but wanted to make his food last as long as possible. He remembered his "Rule of Threes" and knew that his body would be able to survive for a long time, even if he didn't have any food. So, he ate just enough to hopefully keep his energy up.

After 30 minutes or so, Caleb put his boots back on and tied the laces. He rose to his feet and placed the empty bag in the pocket with the other one he had kept. He lifted up the pack, buckled the waist and chest straps, and continued following the water.

•••••

Holman and Tawna sat in her truck and watched as the last of the quads rode back into the parking lot, dust billowing up behind it in its wake. They had all been recalled to the command center to refuel the off-road vehicles, get some rest if possible, and charge up their radios. The results of the search had been fruitless. They hadn't found any tracks that were for sure Caleb's. They didn't encounter any trash or gear left behind, nor had they seen any remnants of a campsite or fire.

Holman wasn't sure if Caleb had brought a lighter with him or not. He couldn't for certain tell Tawna if he had the ability to make fire. In fact, he wasn't sure what Caleb had at all, other than a sleeping bag, a sleeping pad, and the clothes he was wearing.

For campouts the biggest challenge for the leaders, in all honesty, was to just make sure the scouts had sleeping bags, jackets, flashlights, food, and water; everything else was extra. They hoped the boys brought maps, compasses, knives, etc. Hopefully there were some first aid items in their bags along with maybe some matches or a lighter, but they didn't check each boy's belongings. The leaders always carried those items in their packs to ensure sure those things were brought along. They were supposed to be together as a group and that provided safety for all.

"We've heard that the parents are coming out with the Sheriff later tonight," Tawna said and Holman's heart sank. Again, he felt so guilty for having lost their son; Caleb had been his responsibility for the week. They had trusted him and he had failed them. "Don't get all depressed on me," Tawna said, "that would be counterproductive and a waste of energy. Don't put the weight of this on your shoulders. You were one of three leaders and we all know that caring for boys can sometimes be like wrangling cats." They both gave a small, slightly uncomfortable laugh at that and she continued, "Things happen. This happened. You can't do anything to change it, all we can do is try and remedy the situation as quickly as we can."

"I know. I know you're right, but it's still difficult to separate the emotions of what's happening from the logistics of the search," he said.

"I understand. I can sit here and tell you all day not to beat yourself up over this, but the spot you're in is a tough one." They both sat and looked out over the terrain through the dusty windshield. The map of the area was still on the hood of the truck with various camping items weighing down each of the corners. "I guess I should head out and rally the troops," she said as she opened the door and stepped out of the vehicle, leaving Holman inside by himself.

He watched her walk across the front of the truck and then lean on the push guard that extended off of the vehicle. It was one of those large, beefy metal bumpers that protected the truck if it hit a deer or another large animal. She chatted with a couple other searchers and he watched as she pointed off in the distance and made hand gestures as part of their discussion.

"Rescue 5-4, Rescue 1," suddenly came from the radio speaker attached to the dashboard. It was turned up rather loud and caused Holman to practically jump out of his skin. "Rescue 5-4, Rescue 1," the radio said again. Holman picked up the microphone, pressed down the button on the side of it, and said, "Rescue 1, this is Rescue 5-4, please standby." He opened the truck door and called out, "Tawna, they're calling for you on the radio!"

Tawna came back to the cab of the truck and grabbed the mic, "Rescue 1, go ahead."

"Rescue 5-4, Rescue 1, be advised, helo inbound, estimated time of arrival 1500 hours."

"Rescue 1, Rescue 5-4, copy that, helo inbound, ETA of 1500," Tawna replied. The man on the other end of the channel then passed along the call sign of the helicopter and the frequency on which it could be contacted. At the end of the exchange, Tawna hung the mic back on the cradle on the side of the radio control box.

"Helicopter time!" she shouted and gave Holman's upper arm a firm, excited squeeze. "It should be here around three o'clock. Game changer!"

•••••

Caleb was tired. It would still be quite a while until the sun would go down, but the lack of calories was taking its toll on him. He stopped sooner than he had wanted to.

It's not like I have an appointment or anything, he thought to himself.

He looked at the little creek. It was still a nice depth to refill his bottle. He searched up and down the stream for 20 or so yards in each direction and saw no paw prints in the mud. He did see some hoof marks from what he assumed were deer; not anything to worry about.

Despite only seeing the hoof prints, he still went off into the trees about a minute's walk from the water and found a good place to make camp for the night. He sat down and thought about making a shelter. He knew that, after water, shelter was the next most important thing. He didn't want to take time and energy to build one if he was just going to leave it tomorrow though.

As he sat there contemplating the shelter, he heard a soft, rapid *whup-whup-whup* sound. He tilted his head to the side and pointed his ear in what he believed to be the direction the sound was coming from. He thought it might be a woodpecker on the trunk of a tree, or a similar animal. The noise faded and he soon forgot about it. A few minutes passed and it came back again, slightly louder. What was that?

It faded again, but this time it had truly aroused his interest. He stood up and walked to a more open spot between trees and waited. A minute later it returned yet again and this time he knew it wasn't an animal, it was a helicopter! He could tell from the sound that it wasn't close enough to see him. He started yelling and looking up at the sky while waving his arms anyway. Even if it was right on top of him, the pilot would never hear him over the noise of the engines. He didn't know what else to do and he felt like he *had* to do something.

Caleb continued waving. He removed his jacket and began swinging it around in circles over his head and screamed, "I'm here! Help me!" But the helicopter never materialized. After a minute or so the vibration of the large, swirling rotor blades faded away and Caleb again found himself on his knees crying.

That had to have been someone looking for me, it had to be.

DAY 4

The prospect of being rescued the previous evening had sapped Caleb of his energy. He hadn't been sure if he wanted to build a shelter or not, and that was before hearing the helicopter. After the adrenaline spike faded he felt tired, and the decision was essentially made for him. He would not be making a shelter until later. He just didn't have it in him to do so. After recovering from his crying, he had laid out his sleeping arrangements and dipped his bottle into the running water. After a few sips of fresh water he went to sleep. It was the end another exhausting day, both physically and mentally.

Now, he was waking up in the cool morning, and there was a damp smell in the air. He rose and relieved himself at the base of a tree a few yards from his sleeping area. While doing so, he looked up and saw the faint twinkling of the last couple of stars that were yet to be swallowed up in the dawn's growing light. As he looked skyward, he saw, although he could not feel it down on the forest floor where he stood, that there was a slight breeze gently swaying the very tops of the trees.

He zipped up his pants, returned to his sleeping area, and opened up his pack. Reaching inside he removed his remaining half energy bar; he had eaten the first half yesterday afternoon. He was rationing his food as best he could, but it was still running out rather fast. A constant hunger gnawed at him which made the rationing very difficult.

The word "hungry" had definitely taken on a new meaning since becoming lost out in the woods. Back home if he wanted a snack he would say to his mom, "I'm hungry" and his mother would tell him that he wasn't hungry, he just wanted to eat food because it tasted good. "No, mom, I'm really hungry!" he would say and wrap both arms around his stomach and bend over slightly, like he was cramping badly because of his unbearable hunger. She would tell him to stop being ridiculous, that he'd never actually known what it felt like to be truly hungry.

Well, that had changed. He now knew *exactly* what being hungry felt like, and it hurt. He chewed slowly and savored every morsel of the energy bar, but it still left him wanting. He could feel his belly tightening up with cramps as he ate the bar, like his body was telling him that it wanted more. He drank his fill of water to try and top off his empty belly. The first few sips he took actually caused his stomach to clench up even more.

Putting away the wrapper and bottle he looked around, taking in his surroundings a little more thoroughly than he had the day before. He wasn't sure if moving on was the right thing to do, especially after hearing the helicopter. What if instead of getting closer to someone that could help, he was moving farther away? What if his movements took him out of the search zone of aircraft or searchers on the ground?

Maybe I'm already out of the search area. Maybe they're not looking in the right place. These thoughts made his heart sink.

He attempted to gather himself and focus on what actions he needed to take. He thought about what his scout leaders had told him or what he thought they might say if they could talk to him right now. He closed his eyes and tried to channel Mr. Holman.

What do you think you should do if you get lost? came his voice.

Go back to where I last saw my troop or stay still.

Correct, you tried that, but it didn't work out. You kept moving though, why?

I needed to find water. I know I should have stayed where I was, but I had to have hydration.

I understand, no problem. Maybe you ought to have stayed still after finding water, but you moved on and that's okay. Now that you're here, what do you think you should do next?

Mr. Holman, I think I need to make a shelter, but I left my last camp because of the paw prints. I'm worried I haven't moved far enough away.

A shelter is a good idea, you don't know what weather might be coming your way. Staying warm and dry is very important. The camping spot you just left may have been a bear's home turf and it might have been upset that you were in its territory and using its drinking hole. Do you see any paw prints now?

I don't, no.

Are there any other indicators of predators in the area?

Caleb looked around, not sure what else Mr. Holman might be talking about. Then he remembered, he himself had needed to pee several times and animals would too. He thought about it and concluded that he hadn't seen any scat or bear poop, just some smaller nuggets from other animals. Those were probably from deer or maybe bighorn sheep, he didn't really know if any of those were around here.

Do you remember what else bears do to mark their territory?

Caleb's forehead wrinkled as he thought hard about it, and after a moment his memory kicked in. It was like a door to this particular image was unlocked and he saw it, clear as day.

"They scratch up the bark of tree trunks with their claws!" he exclaimed out loud, his face the picture of joy at having found the information, though it resided in a much unused portion of his brain. It was like his mind had hung on to that tidbit of data, but hadn't stored it in a location that was easy to reach.

That's right! Bears stand up on their hind legs and claw into the bark of trees. It's like a NO TRESPASSING sign for other bears.

Caleb scanned the nearby trees looking for deep scratch marks in the bark and didn't notice any, but he didn't think that bears marked up every tree in the area. He set out to check all the trees within approximately a 50 foot radius of where he had slept. This took a while because he needed to circle each tree completely. After a short time, he started getting his trees mixed up and there were some that he couldn't remember if he had looked at already or not. In the end, he more than likely circled several trees twice, but the task was still accomplished and he felt a little safer for it.

No bears, Mr. Holman. I didn't see any large scat either.

Good, great job. So what now?

Caleb thought hard, scrunching his forehead again and squeezing his eyebrows together. His hand instinctively came up to his chin and slowly stroked it. If he had seen a photo of himself in that moment, he would have realized that he was doing the exact same action that his father did when he was problem solving. He finally came up with an idea.

I should try and find a good area for a shelter.

Good thinking, Caleb, that's probably a good idea.

Caleb looked up again and still saw clear skies. Then he remembered the dampness that he had smelled in the air. He sniffed again and got the same sensation. Maybe rain *was* on the way, he just couldn't see it because of the trees.

I should start now, but I'm not quite sure I remember how. Again, he looked for information that was hiding, like it was stored in the attic of his mind just waiting to be discovered and dusted off. *I remember what the drawing of a shelter looks like from our scout book. It's like a tripod with one of the legs being a lot longer than the other. Then I could use tree branches with leaves or thick needles to layer along both sides of the long tripod leg.*

Exactly. So, where are you going to get the legs of the tripod and the fresh branches?

Caleb looked around at his surroundings, hands

resting on his hips, searching for any fallen trees. He saw one a little ways off. It was a tree that had toppled over and its roots were intertwined with the roots of another. When it had fallen over it uprooted the other along with it.

Caleb walked in the direction of the timber and spotted a few branches on the dead tree that he thought might work for the supports of his shelter. He started kicking at them, trying to break them off the trunk. He only succeeded in causing himself to stop after about a dozen kicks, out of breath and with a sore leg. When he had gained his breath back he tried again, but he was not successful. Mr. Holman's voice came into his mind yet again.

Do you think that you're going to be able to break this branch, or will you only wear yourself out? Are you just wasting energy? If so, then maybe you should find another, more easily broken off limb that will do the job.

Caleb heeded the voice of his scout leader and moved on. He wound up finding one of the two shorter branches he needed already broken off and lying next to the second tree he approached. After several more attempts, he eventually found and removed, again by kicking, the other two support branches he needed and dragged them all back to where he planned on making his shelter.

He dropped the tree limbs on the ground, then wiped the bits of bark and dirt that were stuck to his hands on his pants. He began to set them up and soon realized that he would need something to bind the supports together in order to keep the whole structure upright. With hands on hips he started to mentally go through an inventory of what was available to him.

He could use his boot laces, but he really thought he ought to keep those in place and find something else. If he walked around too much in loose boots he might get blisters. He had his belt, but his knife sheath was attached to that and he didn't want to give it up yet. He then spied his jacket lying on top of his hiking pack. Dangling from the lower corners of the opening of the front of the jacket, where the two sides of the zipper came together, he noticed what looked like the ends of shoestrings. He picked up the article of clothing and examined it more closely: they were the ends of the drawstring that ran through the bottom of the garment.

He had never utilized the drawstring and knew it would be put to better use keeping his shelter upright, rather than staying where it was. He removed the knife from his belt and cut the string just inside of one of the knots that was there in order to keep it from accidentally being removed. Once he made the cut, he replaced his knife in the sheath and tugged on the opposite end of the string, removing it from the jacket.

Now that he had a way to secure the branches together, he grasped the two shorter limbs and stood them in a position similar to an upside-down V, crossing slightly at the top. He wrapped the string around the spot where the branches intersected a few times to keep them together and then grabbed the longer one. He set the long branch atop the other two, nestling it into the small crook made by the inverted V. The remainder of the string was then lashed around all three branches, using a method learned in scouts to ensure it stayed tight and secure. Once he reached the end of the line, he tucked it between a couple of the wraps, not wanting to tie a knot he might have to undo later.

Now, time to find lush, green branches to lay along the two sides for cover.

•••••

Holman looked at the expanse of forest through the lower windows of the helicopter and spoke into the microphone of his headset, "That's it right down there, that's where we camped."

The helicopter pilot, sitting in the left seat of the cockpit, nodded at this from behind the tinted visor of his helmet. He pressed the mic button on the stick he was holding to steer the aircraft, "Rescue 5-4, Static 4-1." He released the switch and waited a few moments for a reply.

"Static 4-1, Rescue 5-4, go ahead," came Tawna's voice over the radio.

"Rescue 5-4, Static 4-1, we have arrived at the campsite and will now proceed southbound on the first leg of the search pattern. Will relay any pertinent info as we get it."

"Static 4-1, Rescue 5-4, copy all, good luck."

The helicopter pilot didn't verbally respond to the last transmission, but instead clicked his mic button twice. This was a way of acknowledging a message received without having to talk over the air again, brevity in radio communications is key.

Holman looked out the window to his right, scanning the woods below for any sign of Caleb. He couldn't be very far, he was only a boy and had not filled out with muscle like he would once he got further into his teens. They estimated he may have trekked 8-10 miles in any direction at *most*. Holman guessed that he was well within that distance. The issue was that he was a single person in a large expanse of wilderness without any tools—that they knew of—that he could use to make his presence known to a rescue team.

• • • • •

Caleb's good start on building his shelter earlier in the day petered out soon after the initial victory of lashing together the supports. After the first steps of the setup were completed, he had begun a search for live branches, flush with pine needles. He soon realized that the problem with that was the fact that limbs full of green, insulating needles or leaves were not just laying around on the ground waiting to be picked up or to be broken off of fallen trees. He would have to remove them from living trees.

Caleb only had one cutting tool with him and that was the knife on his belt. It wasn't a small knife, but it wasn't very large either. On top of that, it was a nice, smooth, sharp blade. It was not a gnarly, toothy serrated cutting edge that would act like a saw, which would be perfect for taking branches off of a living tree. Despite not being the preferred sharp edge for the task, he still had to find a way to make it work.

In the beginning, there was not much success to speak of. Regardless of its sharpness, the knife just didn't have the bite that the task required. After expending much time and effort trying to cut some branches, he decided to take a small break. He returned to his sleeping area and sat down on top of his rolled up sleeping bag. He pondered the problem while he sipped water from his container.

While sitting there and searching the recesses of his brain for a solution, he remembered a book he had read not too long ago. The name of the novel was *Hatchet* and it was about a boy, much lie Caleb, who found himself lost and alone in the woods just trying to survive. The book's title came from the fact that the boy had a shiny new hatchet with him, and it proved to be quite the handy tool. With a tool such as that he would be able to chop branches off of trees easily.

From there his mind wandered off. He began to

wonder if the people out there looking for him were close at all. He hadn't heard the *whup-whup-whup* of rotor blades all day and started to lose heart. He missed his family, the thought of maybe never seeing them again caused him to hang his head low, his chin touching his chest.

His mind continued to wander, as minds tend to do, and after a few minutes he was thinking about having a hatchet magically appear next to him. How amazing that would be. It would be just like in a video game, when your character is running along and you come upon different treasures and tools just lying there on the ground, faintly glowing blue to let you know that they're tools to be added to your inventory.

Man, that would be awesome! he thought and smiled. While he was picturing the hatchet in his mind he noticed its sharp, smooth blade.

"Well, I've got a sharp, smooth blade too," he said out loud in a scratchy voice he hadn't used all day, "so why would that tool work and not mine?" He looked closer at his mental image. The hatchet was basically just a blade that was thicker and on the end of a stick.

Caleb rose to his feet and searched out a branch much thinner than the ones he had used for his shelter. He looked for one that was about the thickness of a hammer handle and not rotted out or eaten up on the inside by bugs. Once he found one, it was about the length of both his upper and lower arms combined from shoulder to wrist, he removed one of his boot laces and lashed his knife to the end of the stick. He knew this was a temporary use so didn't mind using the bootlace in this instance.

Once the knife was affixed firmly to the stick, he set out to try again at removing a fresh branch from a tree. He lined the blade up to the area he wanted to strike, right where the limb sprouted out from the tree trunk, and raised the stick above his head, holding it with both hands, and swung it with great force onto the branch.

Thunk! came the dull sound as the blade bounced off the tree. He looked at the place where the knife had struck and saw only a tiny, superficial cut that barely even broke the "skin" of the plant. Undeterred, Caleb repeated the process half a dozen more times and paused repeatedly to inspect his work. Again, just a bunch of cosmetic cuts amounting to no real damage. He was no closer to separating the branch from the tree as the knife just kept bouncing right off. This wasn't working.

Caleb closed his eyes and summoned the image of the hatchet again. What was it that made that tool more effective than his? They were both sharp. They were both attached to the end of a handle so they could be swung easily, adding force to the strikes. His blade was smaller than the hatchet, but so what? Wait...that was it!

"The hatchet is bigger which makes it heavier!" he blurted out loud. He looked down at the knife in his hand and started to unwrap the bootlace that kept it lashed to the stick. Once that was done and the lace was back in its proper place he ditched the smaller branch, flinging it off into the distance. He then began searching, yet again, for the right stick. This time he was in need of a thicker, heavier branch, but not so heavy that he wouldn't be able to swing it one handed.

Once the perfect stick was found he returned to the tree he had been chopping at. He removed the knife from its sheath yet again and held it firmly with his left hand, blade pressed against the flesh of the tree, the sharp edge perpendicular to the limb. He raised the new, larger branch high above his head with his right arm. He paused for a moment and took a steadying breath while closing his eyes. He felt deep inside that this was either going to work, or his hopes of creating a shelter were done for. This was a make or break moment. Caleb opened his eyes, focused on the back of the blade, and swung down as hard as he could onto the knife.

There was a nice, hearty *thup* sound. He looked closely at the result of his action and saw that the blade had cut into the flesh of the tree. Success! The branch he swung had acted much like a hammer onto a nail, the nail in this case being the knife. With the momentum of the "hammer" he was able to make a deep gash into the tree limb.

He swung the large stick five or six more times. Suddenly the branch was laying on the forest floor in front of him, separated from the body of the tree. After staring at the branch for a few seconds in disbelief, he hurriedly rushed to the next limb he had targeted and separated it from the trunk as well. Then on to the next, then the next. There were a few attempts where the branch he was swinging didn't strike the knife blade perfectly and instead of cutting into the tree the blade flipped over onto its side, but he perfected his craft quickly.

After 15 minutes of swinging away he had—what he hoped would be—enough branches to cover both sides of his shelter. Out of breath, he walked over to the side of the shelter structure and set the branches down, sweat dripping off his chin and brow as he bent low to pick up his water bottle. He unscrewed the cap and chugged, some of the water leaking from the corners of his mouth and dribbling down onto the front of his shirt. Once he had drunk his fill, he pulled his shirt up and wiped off his face, leaving a large damp smudge on the fabric. He noticed, for the first time really, the graphic on his t-shirt. It was one he had just pulled out of his dresser drawer absentmindedly while getting ready for the campout. The design was a cartoon Tyrannosaurus Rex wearing a Santa Claus hat and its torso was covered in colored Christmas lights. At its feet were wrapped presents and the large words TREE REX. He chuckled, partially because he thought the shirt was funny, but also because it was late summer and not really the normal time to be sporting Christmas attire.

Caleb took another sip from his bottle, picked up his collection of freshly cut branches, and began arranging them on the sides of the shelter.

DAY 5

After a day and a half of searching by air, Holman was exhausted. Searching with an airplane or helicopter is a fantastic way to cover miles and miles of territory both easily and quickly. However, the majority of the area that he and the pilot had flown over was covered by vegetation. So, not only was he looking for a boy who was dwarfed by just one of the thousands and thousands of trees he was soaring over, but for all he knew he might have flown right over the top of Caleb. There was a good chance that he couldn't see him because he happened to be under one of those trees at the time! It was draining to try and focus his searching eyes for hours on end.

Holman woke up with the sun, ready for his third

day of looking for Caleb, but that plan would soon be thwarted. He rose from his sleeping bag and, exiting his tent, slipped his feet into his boots that were just outside the entrance. He left them untied as he shuffled away from the shelter. He was wearing the same clothes he had been wearing for a week straight now. His nose had become accustomed to the smell so he didn't register it, but he knew he had to smell extremely bad right now to everyone around him. He gave a small, tentative sniff at the shirt he pulled up towards his face and he grimaced.

Whew! I offend myself! In his mind he heard the funny voice he used with the kids when they were acting silly at home.

He approached the large, two-burner stove that was set up at the edge of the camping area in the trailhead parking lot where someone had already heated up water for coffee, hot chocolate, oatmeal...whatever. He mixed a packet of instant brown sugar flavored oatmeal in a bowl and stirred it with a plastic spoon.

"Morning, Holman," came a voice from behind him. Holman turned, looking slightly over his shoulder to see who it was.

"Morning, Tawna. Did you sleep well?" he said.

"Not too bad, not too bad," she replied. She always felt a little bit weird, a little off, having normal, everyday conversations with families when their loved one was either missing or being rescued due to serious injury. It was just human nature though; it wasn't insensitive to try and find relief from all the stress of the situation by seeking out things that brought normalcy back to life. For example, Tawna knew that during wartime soldiers frequently watched movies, read books, played video games, etc. not long after being involved in violent conflict. It wasn't because they didn't care, but it was a way of coping and finding relief from the tough spot they were in. She felt like she could identify with that.

"Holman," she said, "we're gonna be sending you home this morning." Holman froze, eyes on Tawna and his lips parted, a spoonful of steaming oatmeal raised halfway between the bowl in his hand and his mouth. He slowly lowered the spoon.

"What? Why?"

"You need to go and see your family. You've been out here longer than anyone else and you have, in my opinion, burned out. You're tired and we need people who are well rested."

"I am rested, I just woke up!" he said, trying to save his position in the search effort.

"I'm not just talking about sleep," she replied in a calm, soothing voice, "I'm talking about everything that's going on around here, everything. We greatly appreciate your help, but you need to go home, take a shower, and be with your family. They need you more than we need you right now, if I'm being honest."

"Tawna, I get it, I get it," he said, holding up his hands, "but I'm still an asset, I *need* to find this boy." Holman appealed to her with his eyes and she could hear the pleading in his voice. He then exhaled with a low, defeated tone, "He was our responsibility and we lost him." He lowered his arms and looked down at the dust covered toes of his untied boots, his shoulders sagging.

Tawna knew he was pulling on her emotions, and it was working a little bit, but she needed to be reasonable. "Thinking like that isn't going to do you or anyone else any good," she said, regaining her resolve. "We've already talked about that and you hanging this situation on yourself isn't going to help anyone. Stuff like this happens, it's part of life and we need to just deal with it."

After a pause she continued, "We lost the helo for the day. It went back last night, as you know, to refuel. While at the helipad it got called to another rescue effort. Leadership has determined that, at this point, that operation has a better chance of success." Those last words stung Holman, they pricked him right in the heart. The look of sudden shock swept across his face. It was the first time that it truly registered with him that Caleb might not be found. It was always just a matter of time, he had thought, and they would find him.

Caleb's parents were renting a room at a motel not too far away after staying at the campsite their first night. Holman knew they were in the area. He was yet to see them, as they too had gone out searching, though they were conducting their search on the quads. He thought he should linger long enough to see them before he left.

"I'll stay until his mother and father get here and then I'll ride into town and have someone pick me up from there." Tawna looked at him with a contemplating look, then nodded her head and walked away.

•••••

Later in the day Caleb's parents returned to refuel their quads and their empty stomachs as well. They met for a short time with Holman. People who witnessed the interaction clearly saw that they were comforting him instead of the other way around. While the parents were, of course, extremely worried about the welfare of Caleb, they knew that Holman hung the heavy weight of guilt around his neck. He felt completely responsible for the boy getting lost in the first place. They tried to relieve him of some of that weight, but there wasn't much they could do in the moment. The best way to fix everything was to find their son, then everyone would talk about it at family gatherings with words of happiness and relief mixed on their tongues, because it had all turned out okay.

Hey, remember that time one of your scouts got lost and you had helicopters and off-road vehicles and everything out looking for him? Man, that was CRAZY!

After a few minutes of speaking, Holman hugged

each of them individually, then walked to a truck that was going to take him back into town.

Caleb's parents, Carter and Layla, had been married for 14 years and had a daughter as well, Caleb being the older of the two. They had met at church many years ago and hit it off immediately. Over a brief time they went on multiple dates and spoke over the phone almost nonstop. Carter even got in trouble at his job for being on the phone too much and not earning his keep. After a few short months he proposed to Layla, and two months later they were married. They honestly would have gotten hitched sooner, but they wanted to give people time to make travel plans and mark it on their calendars so they could come to the ceremony. Layla and Carter realized that while it was "their day", it's also one of the most monumental days in the lives of their parents and wanted them to have time to make arrangements.

Caleb had heard the story of how his parents met and married dozens of times, usually when they had guests over for dinner. Inevitably one of the guests would comment on getting married after not knowing each other for very long and his dad would always reply, "Well, when you know, you know!"

That was Carter, when he knew something was true or needed to be done, that was it. With Layla, he knew she was the one he wanted to be with forever and saw no sense in delaying. He took action and married her without hesitation. That same mentality had overtaken him now. His son was missing, but instead of curling up into a ball and crying, his way of dealing with it was to get to the rescue base camp and be part of the active effort to find Caleb.

Layla was more reserved, but much the same as Carter. She too wanted to be there on site looking for Caleb. She wanted to help search, obviously, as she was also adept in the outdoors. She had grown up camping in the woods on weekends with her family, sometimes hiking for three days straight, making camp each night in a different location. On one memorable occasion her father had taken her, just her, to the Grand Canyon where they hiked from the South Rim all the way to the North Rim, a total of 24 miles with lots of climbing steep, winding trails. It was her favorite trip of all time and hoped to do the same thing with her kids, but first she had to find Caleb.

Carter and Layla had been out all day riding the quads and had found nothing, not even tracks they could follow. They were not dispirited yet, but they also knew that today was the fifth day that Caleb had been missing and with each passing day his chances of being found alive dropped drastically. Because of this they leaned on their faith. After seeing Holman off and then getting some food and water, they retreated to a wooded area away from everyone else and knelt together. They prayed for the recovery of their son and pleaded that he would be kept safe.

After they returned to the center of the camp, they found Tawna and asked her what the next logical step would be.

"Well," said Tawna, "there're still a couple of hours of daylight, but I feel like we've searched the immediate area really well and searching it again, which is all we have time for before dark, might be a waste of our time." She paused and thought for a moment. Layla could see there was something on her mind that she was struggling to get out.

"What is it Tawna? Just say what it is that you have to say, we don't need to be coddled right now," said Layla in a firm voice, but trying not to sound harsh or ungrateful.

"Alright," Tawna said, "there's not a whole lot we can do other than continue with what we've got, but this can't go on forever," she explained while spreading out her arms and turning, as if displaying all the base camp items and people. "If we don't come up with something new by tomorrow afternoon, we might have to discontinue the search." She scanned their faces for a reaction, but they kept in whatever they were feeling quite well.

After a long moment Carter said, "We understand, you all have your own lives and maybe someone else will need your resources." Tawna was thankful for this response as it made this, one of the more difficult parts of the job, a little bit easier.

"I'm hoping we can get the helo back for tomorrow as searching from the air is such a great tool, but I'm not counting on it," she said. "If we don't get it, we'll just keep up on the ground search with the quads."

Carter thought about this for a minute, "I might be able to get some outside help, let me call someone." He moved over to the table where the satellite phone sat and pulled out his own cell phone. Tawna and Layla could tell that he was scrolling through the contacts on the screen and then he punched the number he found into the larger satellite phone. He held the handset up to his ear and it looked like a black brick with a short, fat antenna sticking up from it.

"I think he's calling our friend Dougie," Layla said to Tawna, while keeping her eyes on her husband. "Carter is an aerospace engineer and has several friends that have private pilot licenses and some that even own small planes. Dougie is one of those guys and probably won't hesitate to bring his plane out here, as long as he's in town and not on vacation or something."

"If he can arrange that it would be fantastic," said Tawna, also watching Carter, her arms folded across her chest.

After a few minutes, Carter removed the satellite phone from the side of his head and punched a button to end the call. He placed it back on the table where he had picked it up from and, while returning his cell to his vest pocket, walked back to where the women were standing.

"That was Dougie," Carter said with a smile, "he said that he'll be able to bring his plane up. He didn't ask for any help with gas money, but I figure we can take up a collection to cover that."

"I can ask my sister to head that up," said Layla, "she's been asking what she can do to help and I'm sure she can set up a fundraising account and then spread the word about it."

"Sounds good, can you call her now?" asked Carter. Layla nodded her head and started to walk over to the table. As she passed her husband, she slowed for a second and reached out her left arm, giving a small squeeze to his forearm. It was the first sign of affection that Tawna had seen since their arrival. She didn't believe there were any issues between them based on what she had observed, but they had been all business since they got to the base camp.

•••••

HELP.

All day long Caleb had been working on spelling out, in large block letters, the word HELP. Not too far from his shelter he had found an area that was moderately open. One might even call it a meadow, but that brings to mind images of birds flittering about as butterflies and insects hop from flower to flower in a sun kissed, grassy paradise. In this case, it was just dirt and rocks. It was assuredly not a place that would serve as the backdrop for an upcoming live action film version of Fern Gully.

The area was open, however, so Caleb decided it was his best option to signal for assistance. He prayed that searchers were still looking for him by air, but all he could do was hope. He thought back to his scouting handbook and the color illustrations showing ways to signal for help when lost or in need. He could see in his mind's eye the image that showed a scout reflecting the sun off of a handheld mirror which could be seen from the air miles and miles away—he had no mirror or anything close. He remembered a boy placing damp or green leaves and bushes onto an already existing fire to create smoke which could be seen from far away—Caleb had no lighter or matches and his attempts at rubbing sticks together this morning had been futile at best. He also had a recollection of a drawing that illustrated scouts making a giant X out of neon colored fabric to be seen from the air—where those kids got that much bright colored fabric in the woods he had no idea. He even remembered a scout shooting a flare up into the sky, a safe distance from any trees that might catch on fire, of course.

"Seriously? What kind of camp leader would allow kids to take flares?" he said in an audible voice filled with doubt.

Caleb had nothing that would help him signal in this situation. So, he had resolved to use what was around him to make a sign. Though not as effective as smoke or neon signs, he knew if he made it big enough it might be seen. Also, he needed to make letters that had sharp right angles, something that would clearly indicate human presence and not something that could be mistaken as an abnormal natural occurrence.

Caleb had spent all morning, and into the afternoon, arranging the rocks and timber that he found lying nearby. He started out by placing small branches and rocks on the ground where the letters would be and then began the task of building them up to a thickness that he hoped could and would be seen from the air. He stopped frequently to drink water and refill his bottle. In the early afternoon he also took time to lie down in the shade of his shelter. Working in the sun was tiring work, but more fatiguing was the fact that he was now 100% out of food.

The food had run out the day before, and that was with him barely eating anything. Now, he had nothing. He had no wire available or anything of the sort to make snares out of. In addition, he wasn't too confident that he'd be able to make an effective snare anyway, so it didn't sting too much. He had, however, found a bush with berries on it, but was afraid to eat them as they were colored bright red. He couldn't remember for sure, but he thought that being an intense color like that meant that they could be poisonous. In the end, he was exhausted and hungry, still he had to keep working.

While he was moving rocks and branches—and anything else he found suitable to pile onto the shapes of letters—he kept having to pull up his pants. At one point he stopped his work and he used his knife to make a new hole in the leather belt he was wearing. With that done he was able to keep working, his pants now cinched up tighter.

As the day wore on, his progress became slower and slower. Not only was his energy waning, but each trip out into the woods meant he had to venture father and farther out as whatever materials had been close to the meadow were already part of the letters. By early evening he had neither heard nor seen any sign of aircraft searching for him and he became depressed and his mind started turning against him. Up until today he had kept a positive mental attitude about his situation, he knew it was a key to survival. Now, though, he just couldn't stop the negative thoughts from seeping, similar to smoke slowly penetrating around the edges of a closed door, into his mind.

They're never going to find you, came a sinister voice in his head that sounded much like his. *They've already given up.* Caleb currently didn't have the heart or mental strength to counter the voice and it continued speaking.

They looked for you, but they can't look forever. The people searching for you have families too and they can't be out here trying to find you until the end of time. You're just a kid. They probably assume you've been eaten by a mountain lion or bear, or maybe fallen off a cliff by now.

With the weight of the thought that he might never be found weighing down on him, Caleb sat down on the ground and slumped over onto his side and cried. It wasn't a weeping and wailing cry, just a sad, soft whimper accompanied by tears that pooled in the little dip between his eye and the bridge of his nose. Eventually they overflowed and fell to the dirt beneath his head.

You can cry all you want, but they're not coming. They're probably at home right now playing out the classic lost child scene from movies and TV. You know the one, right? The dad's in the garage or yard working to fix something since he can't fix the fact that his son is dead and he never even found a body to bury. Mom, however, she's in your room sitting on your impeccably made bed with her feet resting on the tidy floor. In her perfectly manicured hands she's holding your favorite stuffed animal and crying while staring at it and stroking its dirty, worn fur with her hands. Your aunt is standing in the hallway just outside of the doorway with her arms folded tightly across her chest, looking at your mother and wondering what she should do to comfort her. Yep, that's happening right now, because you're already gone. They've accepted that they'll never find you.

Caleb continued laying on his side, still overcome with sadness, though his tears were already subsiding. He thought about sitting up, but it felt like the weight of a large animal was resting on him.

You know what Caleb? They might not even be doing those things, they might have already moved on. Even now, your sister is moving your stuff out of your room so she can move hers in. You did have the larger room after all. She's also excited that she doesn't have to stop watching her favorite shows when it's your turn to be in charge of the TV.

An image of Amber, his younger sister by two years, carelessly throwing his stuff into a cardboard box entered his mind. She would take the box out to the curb to leave it next to the trash cans for pick up.

Yeah, I'm confident that's actually what is going on right now. In fact, I'm pretty sure that your parents never wanted a boy at all. Now they're finally getting the family they always wanted, just them and Amber.

Caleb's eyes, which had closed by now, snapped open at that last train of thought. His breath caught in his chest and, after a slight pause, he raised himself up quickly, throwing the imaginary animal off of him.

"That's not true," he said out loud. "None of that is true!" he yelled, his voice echoing into the quiet forest around him. The voice didn't come back, and he hoped that it had gone for good.

He raised himself up to his feet, but immediately sat back down as he got lightheaded when he did so. He remained there with his arms resting on his knees and looked over towards his shelter.

"I need to eat," he said, "that's why I'm having these bad thoughts." He got to his feet, but much slower this time, and avoided getting lightheaded again. He walked over to where he had seen the red berries on the bush, and stood there for a moment looking at them.

Are you going to eat those? Said a voice in his head, but this time it was that of his leader, Mr. Holman.

I don't know. I want to. I need to eat something or I'll be too weak to do anything.

Well? What do you think? How can you know if they're poisonous or not?

I can't without tasting them, I guess.

So, it comes down to how bad do you need them for food?

Caleb reached out and plucked a berry from one of the branches and slowly rolled it between his thumb and index finger while staring at it, contemplating the small fruit. He raised it to his nose and gave a good sniff. It didn't give off an odor that was either sweet or bitter. He stared at it for a minute longer while holding it in front of him in his open palm.

Finally, he closed his hand tightly over the red berry and he felt a small *pop* beneath his fingers as the sphere...well, popped. He opened his hand and, without hesitation, gave a tiny lick with his tongue to the burst berry splotch. He didn't swallow, but held in his mouth the little bit he had licked up. He swished it around with some saliva.

Well? said Mr. Holman's voice.

It's a little sweet, clearly not bitter. I'm gonna just hold it in my mouth a little longer.

Not a bad idea.

After a couple of minutes Caleb spit out the mix of saliva and berry juice, some of it dribbling onto his chin. It was most definitely not the best tasting berry he had ever had, despite his real hunger, but it wasn't bitter; his mouth didn't feel numb or tingly. Maybe they were edible!

So what's your plan now? If you're going to eat them you shouldn't eat too many. They might still be bad for you and make you sick. Or maybe, since you haven't eaten anything in a while, they might make you sick anyways.

Caleb thought on the advice that his leader's voice was giving him as he reached out to the bush again. This time his hand came back with about ten or so berries. He held them in his cupped hand and shook them gently, causing them to bump against one another like he was getting ready to roll some dice.

With his free hand he plucked up three from the group and popped them into his mouth. The flavor explosion he experienced while chewing was beyond what he expected based on the berry taste test he had performed. He closed his eyes, tilted his face towards the sky, and moaned with pleasure. This was the best thing he had ever eaten in his life! He chewed slowly and savored every bit of flavor he could get out of the food before swallowing. He then ate four more berries, then the rest. The taste was so great that he started swaying on his feet and, quite literally, could not stop making small moans and grunts of pleasure while savoring the flavor.

When he had finished the berries, it took all of his willpower to not reach out and pick more of them. He needed to stick to his plan of not gorging, reducing his chances of getting sick. He turned on his heel and walked away before the temptation became too strong for him to resist.

When he got back to his shelter, he drank from his water bottle and then refilled it at the stream. He screwed the cap back into place and set it on top of his backpack, where it was still leaning against a tree. Even though he had only eaten a very small amount, he felt absolutely rejuvenated. This was due to the mental relief that he had been able to find a food source that seemed edible, but also from the influx of sugary calories he had gotten from the meal.

It had been a long, tiring day for him, and he still had a lot of work to do on his HELP letters. He sat down on the end of his sleeping bag beneath his shelter and removed his boots. It wasn't dark yet, but he didn't feel like returning to the task. He laid back onto his sleeping bag and stared up at the underside of his little roof. Pinholes of light broke through the crisscrossing of the branches and needles. He laced his fingers together and put his hands beneath his head. He continued to look at the pinholes of light, trying to create images out of them, like people have done for thousands of years when making constellations out of groups of stars in the night sky. After a short while of playing this little game, Caleb's eyes closed without him noticing and soon he was fast asleep.

DAY 6

Carter and Layla both rose with the sun the next day and, after eating a quick breakfast, were once more ready to head out with a group of searchers on the quads. They packed plenty of water and food with them for the day, but were unfortunately limited by the need for fuel. Carter, though, had filled up four gallon-sized gas containers and used bungee cords to secure two jugs each onto their all-terrain vehicle's cargo racks. They were ready to go all day.

They each slipped their motorcycle helmets on, tightened the chin straps, and mounted their vehicles. After everyone had started up their engines, they headed into the forest. Once they had gone a few miles in they would break off into two separate groups to search different areas. Periodically, Carter would glance up to the sky. Dougie would be flying in today, but he wasn't sure when exactly he would be arriving, nor did he know if he would even fly over the area he happened to be searching in. He'd be there though, hunting from the air for Caleb with the rest of them.

•••••

Caleb rose early as well, and, while his parents were eating their quick meal, he too was having breakfast. He woke up not having experienced any negative effects from the berries he had eaten the previous day, so after he got up and slipped on his boots he went straight to the berry bush. He filled his hat up with several handfuls of the fruit. There were still plenty to be had on the branches, but not enough so that he could eat very well for very long. He would need to locate other berry bushes or something else to eat.

For the time being, though, he headed back to his sleeping area and stuffed his face with food and drank healthy amounts of water from his bottle. He couldn't see it, but he could feel the remnants of berries all over his lips. He rose to his feet and pulled up his pants again—he would soon need to make another notch on the belt—and walked over to the stream. Kneeling down at the edge of the water, he cupped some into his hands and gave his face a light washing, first splashing water up onto his dirty skin and then rubbing his damp palms all over. He did this several times until, he hoped, most of the berry bits and dirt was gone from his face. His mom would be so proud. When he finished with the washing, he refilled his bottle, stood up, tightened his boots, and made his way back to the meadow to work on his HELP sign.

When he arrived back at the open field, he looked at his creation from the previous day and was a little bit deflated. The strength and confidence he was feeling this morning, a result of the good night's rest and the big breakfast he had eaten, was swept away when he saw just how little work he had actually completed. He realized that in his energy depleted state, although he was putting forth his best effort, he was, in reality, not moving very fast at all.

He had worked very diligently to form giant letters that could be seen from the air. Now the realization struck him, unfortunately, that the letters were nowhere near to being large enough. As with many projects, it is a good idea to step away or take a break from the task after working on it for a bit, then come back to it later. It enables you to see mistakes you might be making that you may not have seen otherwise if you hadn't taken that break. He was now looking at his handiwork through refreshed eyes and what lay before him was a half-formed HELP, with the bottom part of each of the character still missing. Not only that, but the letters were not even close to being oversized enough to realistically be seen from the air, unless the aircraft was really low, like *really low*.

With his hands on his gaunt hips he stood there staring at the previous day's results while lightly chewing on his lip. If his mother could see him right now she would tell him that he looked *exactly* like his maternal grandmother at that moment. Layla's mom had always stood in that same stance, chewing on that lip of hers, when she was "thinking on something" as she had liked to say when pondering a problem. Sadly, Caleb's grandmother had died while he was still a baby, but Layla loved seeing that he had somehow inherited this trait from her. It was something she wouldn't have thought possible, had it not been for the fact that Caleb never knew his grandma long enough to copy her actions, but still had some of her mannerisms.

After a few moments of thinking he came to some conclusions:

1) He needed to make a much larger formation.

2) He was already running out of sign-making materials that were in the immediate area surrounding the meadow.

3) He would need to venture out further and further to find more supplies to finish what he had started, not to mention make the whole thing bigger.

4) Venturing out farther would mean it was going to take a lot longer to finish the project. Also, he would be expending much more valuable energy to complete less and less.

5) Because of the previous four points, he decided he was going to rearrange what he had already collected

into a large X, like he had seen in his scouting handbook. The large letter would just as easily attract the eyes of searchers from above as an entire word would. Humans recognize perfectly straight lines and right angles as something that does not often occur naturally out in the world, and it would act as a signal to human presence. The word HELP would be nice, but he knew that people were already looking for him, he just needed to let them know where he was.

Caleb set to work right away. It was still cool out as the sun hadn't yet risen too far overhead. He noticed the chirps of birds calling to each other and could practically smell the dampness in the meadow air as the little bit of moisture resting on the blades of grass evaporated in the increasing temperature. He also heard what he thought was the faint buzz of bees somewhere nearby. He made a mental note to check it out later. If it was bees he was hearing, he might be able to get some honey! For now, though, he would keep working in the nice morning air.

Steady progress was made on the reconfiguration of the rocks and branches. He made sure the lines were thicker than he thought was necessary because he knew that from far up they would still look thin. When he had finished disassembling and reassembling the materials he had already gathered, he thought that it was much more serviceable. The length of the X's lines could definitely be extended, but he believed the mark was large enough and striking enough to be seen from the air without needing to be enlarged. He would come back tomorrow and double check and see if he was still of the same opinion.

•••••

Caleb's parents had been out searching on the quads for several hours now and had stopped to take a break. They were both seated on the ground with their backs leaning up against the vehicle that Carter had been driving, one against each wheel. Both of them were silently chewing on an energy bar and staring off into the distance, not focusing on anything in particular. They were the perfect picture of being 'lost in thought'.

Layla was remembering Caleb as a toddler, playing with Play-Doh, creating unidentifiable food from his "secret recipes". Layla sat with him at those times, letting him take her order and then pretending to take bites, exclaiming out loud to him how delicious everything was. She thought fondly of how excited he was when Carter brought him to the hospital to meet Amber, his new baby sister. Layla's favorite photo, still hung by a magnet and displayed on the side of the refrigerator with the rest of the kid's artwork from school, was of Caleb sitting in Carter's lap while he held Amber. She could see in the photo the desire for the boy to hold and keep the baby safe from falling, while at the same time not wanting to squeeze the fragile child too hard.

Now that the kids were older, the love and tenderness that was shown in that captured moment wasn't so evident. The two of them seemed to be looking for reasons to fight all of the time and it was trying on her and Carter, but she knew it would pass as it had with her and her siblings. There were plenty of times, however, that she would walk by one of their rooms and peek in to see them lying side by side on one of the beds playing a game or maybe see one of them helping the other with homework or a project. It was in those moments that Layla's heart soared, that she knew that she and Carter were doing a good job raising their children.

Layla was suddenly overcome with sadness, it felt to her as if a hole had opened up in the bottom of her belly and her stomach was now falling through it. She was so afraid that she would never see Caleb again here on this earth, that they would only be able to talk about and remember the memories that were already there and not have the chance to create new ones. She tilted her head back and leaned it against the tire of the quad and moaned at the prospect of having to see the sheer heartbreak in her daughter's eyes if they had to tell her that her brother was never going to be coming back home.

These thoughts were so overwhelming that she was sapped of the little energy needed to remain sitting up. The half energy bar still in the torn wrapper tumbled from her fingertips to the dirt and she slumped over to the ground, curling up onto her side and hugging her knees to her chest. She let loose every emotion of sadness and fear and loss that she had managed to keep at bay, while she and everyone else went about the task of looking for a lost boy, a living boy! Now she was terrified that their search would soon turn into one of looking for the remains of a boy, *her* boy.

She realized that Carter had slumped over on top of her hips and legs and was hugging them tightly to himself. He too was crying. She wasn't sure if her sobbing had prompted this or if it was the other way around. Either way, they were both coming to accept the possibility that their search might not turn out the way that they hoped. They understood, despite all of their desperate, pleading prayers, along with those of many other people, that God might have other plans for their son that did not mesh with their heart's desires.

Minutes passed and, eventually, they had cried out all the tears their bodies were willing to give up at that time. Once the emotions of the moment subsided, they both were overcome with intense fatigue, a tiredness that was so strong that they just didn't have the energy to sit back up. They lay there, letting the tears on their faces dry, leaving behind trails of cleansed skin where the tears had passed through a film of dust. They were the perfect picture of defeat.

After a few minutes had come and gone, Layla gently patted Carter on the shoulder and he sat up, allowing her to do the same. They stayed there, leaning against the quad, and composed themselves. Layla was always shocked at how helpful a good cry could be, but also at just how tired she would be afterwards, even if the episode only lasted a few minutes. The release of all those emotions had been a great relief, but it had also left them exhausted.

"We need to get going again," said Carter, summoning up all his strength and starting to get up, "Caleb is still out there and he needs us to find him."

"Yes," was all Layla said in reply and she quickly replaced the motorcycle helmet over her messed, dirty hair, allowed Carter to help pull her up to her feet, and remounted the vehicle. No matter how tired they were, they needed to keep going. The two of them fired up the engines and Carter went forward a few yards, did a quick U-turn, and pulled up alongside his wife. He messed with the choke on his quad's throttle for a minute to get the best gas mixture for the engine. They looked at each other through the face masks of their helmets and Layla extended her hand out to Carter. He placed his hand in hers and they both squeezed and looked into each other's eyes. After a few moments they released their grip, flipped down the visors on their helmets, and zoomed off into the woods to continue the search.

•••••

Caleb had returned to the berries and filled his hat again after rearranging his sign in the meadow. He had sat down and leaned up against the tree just outside the mouth of his shelter. He enjoyed the berries yet again and washed down their wonderfully sweet taste with fresh water from the stream. With his belly full and tired from the physical work this morning he was ready for a nap, although he doubted that it was even noon yet. He didn't care though, he wasn't on a schedule, he didn't have school or sports practice to get to, he was on 'Lost in the Forest' time! He laughed out loud to himself.

It felt good to be full, to be working, to be *surviving!* Caleb was still scared, but he felt deep down, he *knew*, that he could survive this ordeal and that he would be reunited with his family.

"Take that, you stupid negative thoughts," he said out loud with a smile, remembering the bad state of mind he had been in two days before when he was starving. He looked at his shelter, then looked off in the direction of his large X, then swept his gaze to the empty hat sitting in his lap that rested at his berry stained fingertips. He was still smiling when he closed his eyes and tilted his face to the sky and let out a primal yell, "YAAAAAAAAAAAARRrrrrg!!"

"I can do this, I can do this," Caleb kept saying to himself with his eyes still closed and the back of his head resting against the trunk of the tree, which was hard, but also somehow soft. A few minutes later he was asleep, still wearing his berry stained smile.

Caleb woke in the early afternoon. He was well rested, but unfortunately he now had a horrible crick in his neck from sleeping in such an awkward position. Awkward, what a weird word.

"Awkward, awk-ward, ahhhk-wooooord," Caleb said to himself. "Man, that is the *perfect* word, the word itself is awkward!" he continued with a laugh. "It sounds funny and it's spelled funny too," he said as he envisioned the letters in his mind. "Aaaaahhk-wooooooor-duh". He was giddy. He thought about it.

Man, was there something in those berries? He didn't know, but if the side effect was acting like he had just had a dose of laughing gas instead of oh, you know, DYING, then he would take it.

He slowly walked over to the stream and washed his hands in the cool water. While he did that, and also while he dried his hands on the legs of his pants, he thought about the berry bush. There were possibly enough berries for one more hat full and then that was it, for now anyway. He had no idea how quickly the plant would grow more fruit. He needed to find more of those bushes, but he hadn't seen any more during his collecting of materials for his sign. There had to be more, there was no way this was the *only* berry producing bush in the forest, but he was also not too keen on wandering too far from his camp. He didn't want to wander back into bear territory or be the kid who got lost while being lost!

Then he remembered hearing the buzzing earlier this morning while working in the meadow. He made his way over to the open area and stood out in the clearing. He remained still and listened for a few moments, then he heard it. He slowly turned his head, with his eyes closed, in an effort to get a better idea of where the noise was radiating from. When he had a good sense about where it was coming from, he walked in that direction to the edge of the meadow, and then repeated the exercise. He did this once more and then reached the source of the loud humming. Hanging on the underside of a branch about 10 feet above the ground was a beehive. It didn't look anything like the beehives he had seen in coloring books or cartoons growing up, but it was definitely a beehive.

The yellow and black striped insects flew in and out of and all around the hive, making quite the racket. Now that he was standing just a dozen or so feet away the buzzing was deafening. It was, what he thought to be, a huge hive and there had to be a hundred bees swarming around the outside of it. Who knew how many were still inside with the queen?

Is the queen bee even real? The beehive doesn't appear like any beehive I've ever seen in drawings, so is the queen a fake thing too? He would have to find out after he was back home.

Caleb had never read anything about bees in his scouting handbook or any other book, so he wasn't sure at all about how to tackle the task of getting honey from the beehive. It turns out the best way to approach the hive is to make a small smoky fire and use the smoke to subdue the bees, to keep them from attacking the person invading their space. Caleb, however, didn't have anything to make fire with or know-how on how to make a fire from natural materials, so he wouldn't have been able to smoke out the bees even if he had this knowledge.

He stood there thinking, again with his hands on his hips and chewing lightly on his lower lip, which was now getting chapped after spending all this time outside in the dry air without any lip balm. This problem wasn't an easy one to tackle and he remained there like that for quite some time. He ultimately came to the conclusion that there was no way to get honey from the hive without being attacked by the bees, but if he could minimize the stings it might be worth it.

Caleb made his way back to his camping area and started going through his items. He picked up his jacket and put it on, then pulled a t-shirt over his head, but stopped pulling it down when the collar rested on his nose just below his eyes. When he was younger he and his neighborhood friends would wear their shirts like this sometimes, with only their eyes showing, pretending they were ninjas. He grabbed his hat and yanked it down so that it covered his ears and then picked up his gloves. Marching back to the beehive he thought through his plan once again.

Okay, I'm gonna be completely covered except for my eyes. I'm gonna have my knife out and I'm going to run up to the hive, hack off a big chunk, then then get out of there as fast as I can. As he thought about this he realized he had missed a vital item. *CRAP! I can't reach the hive.*

Even when Caleb extended his arm straight up above his head he topped out at seven feet tall, with the length of the knife that reached up to maybe seven and half feet. That left him at least a foot and a half short of the bottom of the beehive. He needed something to stand on. Luckily the hive was tucked up on the underside of the branch right where it sprouted out from the trunk of the tree. This would enable him to lean something against the tree itself and he wouldn't have to make a free-standing stool or ladder.

Caleb began shedding off the "armor" he was wearing and placed it on the ground at his feet. No sense in taking it off at his camp just to bring it back here later when he had constructed his ladder. He added his jacket to the pile of clothing and then turned on his heel and headed back to the meadow. He concluded that instead of searching for thick, straight branches to use for the ladder that he would just go back to the X and pick out pieces he had already assembled.

He picked over the gathered materials for about 10 minutes before he had the five limbs he hoped would do the trick. He carried three shorter branches in his left arm and he tucked the ends of two longer ones up under his right arm, squeezed them against his torso, and dragged them along behind him. The longer pieces were only about four to five feet long, but it was easier for him to move them this way.

He dropped his cargo next to his discarded clothing and close to the buzzing of the bees. Now he needed to lash the branches together to form his short ladder. He had the two long pieces which would be vertical supports of the contraption and then he would need to attach the shorter ones horizontally as the steps of the ladder. It was a fairly simple project, but the problem he faced was he needed something to lash the pieces together. Each step of the ladder would require two lashings, so six total. He counted up in his head what he already had.

I've got two from my boot laces. I can unwrap the drawstring from my jacket that I used to tie the shelter supports together and then put it back once I'm done with the ladder. Actually, the drawstring is long enough, I think I can cut it in half and make it into two lashings and then tie them back together again for the shelter. I could use my belt for one of the lashings too. That leaves just one more I need. He paused and contemplated what he could use.

Caleb strode back to his hiking pack and stood there looking at it with his hands on his hips. He leaned over and turned the pack around so that the side with the shoulder and waist straps were facing him. He didn't want to cut any of the straps off of the pack, but it might be his only choice. If he ever left this area, he'd want a functioning bag to wear, so he definitely couldn't cut either of the shoulder straps. The chest straps that connected the two shoulder straps weren't long enough for what he needed. That only left the thicker waist strap. That strap's function was to take a large amount of the weight of the backpack off of the shoulders and rest it on the hips.

Well, I'm not carrying any camping stoves, or fuel, or shovel, or anything like that. I just have my sleeping bag, sleeping pad, my bowl, and spoon. That's not much weight at all, I think I'll be just fine without the waist strap should I need to bug out of here.

With that he pulled his knife from the sheath on his hip and cut away the two halves of the waist strap, cutting as close to where they attached to the bag as possible, without slicing the bag itself. He separated the strap from the large pad that was there to provide cushion on the hips. Once that was done, he tied the two ends together in a square knot so they would form a piece long enough to serve their purpose.

For almost two hours Caleb attempted to fasten all the pieces together and eventually he had, what he hoped would be, a serviceable ladder. He found that the biggest obstacle in the ladder making process was tying the pieces together tight enough. Several times he thought he was good and gave the structure a try, only to have it crumple sideways under his weight. When he finally had the lashings as tight as he could get them, he decided it was time to give it a go. I was time to get some honey!

Caleb donned his protective outfit yet again and picked up the ladder, carrying it towards the beehive. As he approached the tree, he slowed down in an effort to not alarm the bees. His heart was beating really fast, he could feel his pulse throbbing in his neck. He had begun sweating, more from being anxious about what he was about to do than from being covered head to toe. He knew he wasn't allergic to bee stings, but the one time he had been stung in his life...man did it hurt!

He was stung when he was younger, and his sister was still a baby at the time. Caleb's dad had filled a kiddie pool in the backyard of their house for the kids to cool off in and play. He remembered the pool vividly as it was blue with cartoon fish printed all over the bottom. Caleb was excited to swim in the water, but his baby sister wouldn't have anything to do with it, she was scared of the printed fish! While Caleb was swimming the family hadn't noticed that the water had also attracted some bees and one of them stung him. It was not a pleasant memory.

He wanted that honey though, and he was going to get it. He closed his eyes and envisioned in his mind again what he was going to do.

I'm gonna slowly climb the ladder, knife in my right hand, and steady myself with my left on the tree trunk. On the top step I'm going to slowly, SLOWLY, reach out with my left hand and gently grab the piece of the hive I'm going to cut off. I'll then start slicing with the knife and then get out of there fast. If the bees begin stinging, I'm just gonna try and break off a chunk, go down the ladder, and run as quickly as I can into the meadow. Probably screaming. Caleb inhaled deeply, pushed the breath out, and started up the ladder.

He proceeded exactly as he had planned it out in

his mind: knife in right hand, left hand steadying himself, moving slowly. As he stepped up from the second step to the third, he heard the buzzing of the bees increase in volume, they definitely did not like his presence. He carefully ascended up to the top step and turned his torso so that it was facing directly at his target.

As he touched the hive, and then raised the knife up from his side, the bees finally came to the conclusion that Caleb really was a threat and they came at him. They looked like a squadron of alien fighter ships sent out to defend the mother ship. They flew all around his arms and head, but for the moment only landed on the hands and arms that were extending towards their home. Caleb was waiting for the first sting to penetrate his skin, but it didn't come. The covering he had put on was working!

He stabbed at the hive about six inches from the bottom edge and sliced downward. If the bees weren't mad yet, man were they ticked off now! More bees poured out of the hive, they were ready for all-out war. They struck their first blow against Caleb when, as he reached out to make his second cut, a bee found its mark on some exposed flesh between the end of the jacket sleeve and one of his gloves. The insect plunged its stinger into the boy's skin and Caleb's wrist was immediately on fire. The pain was way more intense than Caleb remembered it being.

The discomfort made him move faster, he needed

to switch up his slow and methodical movements to more of a hit and run style; the stealth mission had lost all of its stealthiness. He quickly jabbed his blade into the beehive to make his second cut, rapidly sliced down, and immediately replaced the knife back against the side of the hive to make the final horizontal cut connecting the previous two cuts.

The instant he touched the hive, he sensed a pain in his right eye that was utterly shocking. The skin around the eye was aflame, the eyeball itself felt like molten metal had been poured onto it. He grabbed for his face with both hands and, in the process of doing so, leaned over too far. He was blinded by the pain, deafened by the buzzing in his ears, and he could feel himself free falling through the air. It was the first time in his life that he experienced slow motion.

Many people who get into accidents speak later about how, in the moment, everything seemed to take on a sluggish pace, real life suddenly turned into what looked like a slow motion shot from a movie or television show. They were also able to remember many small details about what was going on around them, it seemed their mind went into hyper-awareness mode right before whatever impact happened.

Caleb felt this now, although he didn't know it was a known phenomenon among scientists and most of the population. He didn't remember seeing anything in detail, as his eyes were shut in agony and his hands were still covering his face, but he still felt like the ladder tipping out from underneath him and his fall was slowed down. It seemed like his descent took minutes and minutes before he crashed down to the earth below the hive. Misery encompassed his whole being, no longer just his eye. He landed on his shoulder and the side of his head first, followed by a crushing blow to his right hip, and then the worst pain he had ever felt in his life in his thigh as his legs slammed down into the dirt.

It took all of his power to roll onto his back. He took two deep breaths, was struck by an ache in his chest, felt extremely light-headed, and then passed out.

•••••

Caleb awoke in darkness. When he had begun his attempt at gathering honey it was late afternoon and now it was totally dark, except for a fingernail of a crescent moon which, at the moment, he couldn't see because of all the trees in the way. His sight of the night sky was also hindered by the fact that he could only see out of his left eye, his right one being mostly shut because it was so swollen.

He bit a fingertip on the glove on his left hand between his front teeth and gently pulled his hand out. His wrist still ached from being stung earlier, but it was nothing like his face. With his exposed fingertips he softly, *softly*, probed the flesh around the eye. He could feel the slight prick of the stinger still poking out of his skin right at the outside corner of the eye. He was relieved to know that a bee hadn't actually stung him in the eye itself, but struck right next to it instead. He carefully pinched the stinger with his fingernails and plucked it out, sending more pain through his face and down his spine.

Caleb tried moving his right arm which, though painful and difficult because the right side of his head and his right shoulder had taken the brunt of the fall, he was able to do. He felt the right side of his face and from what he could tell he wasn't bleeding, but it felt like he would have dirt and pine needles embedded into his skin forever.

Caleb needed to decide what action he should take next. He laid his hand back down by his side and just breathed deeply through is nose for a few minutes. When he moved his hand again his thumb brushed his pant leg and he could feel that it was sticky.

Great, I smashed the honeycomb I risked life and limb to get, now I won't even be able to enjoy that. Well, it should still taste good. He lifted his hand back up to his face and licked the fingertips of his glove, happy to have this little pleasure. What he tasted, however, was not honey.

The sticky substance on his glove tasted salty but also like...metal? He didn't know how else to describe it, but that pretty well summed it up. Salty metal...really weird.

What could it be? He tried to pick his head up to

look, but the pain in his head, neck, and shoulders was too much. He bit down on the fingertip of his right glove and removed it the same way he had taken off the other and reached back down to his thigh.

Now that he was feeling his leg with his actual fingertips, not through the glove, he realized that his pants were completely soaked with the sticky substance. It covered the entire side of his thigh. He kept moving his hand up the pant leg to just a few inches below his hip when he bumped into something, something hard...something that caused a lightning strike of pain in his leg when touched. Caleb resolved to push through the discomfort in his neck and lift his head to get a look at what it was.

With all his strength and determination, he picked his head up off the dirt until his eyes were high enough to see over the pair of gloves that now rested on his chest. There he could see, in the muted light provided by the billion stars of the clear night sky and the day old crescent moon, the faint glimmer of shiny metal and polished wood. Caleb could see the handle of his knife sticking straight up out of his thigh. At that sight Caleb's eyes, or more accurately his eye, shot wide open, his eyelid fluttered, and his head dropped back onto the turf. He had just passed out for the second time that day.

•••••

Despite a full day of searching, Carter and Layla returned to the camp empty handed. They were both tired and covered in dust as well as had what were referred to as 'saddle sores'. They had been riding quads all day for three days in a row now, and neither of them, though they had experience riding, had ridden in a long time and their butts just weren't used to it. After the first whole day they were extremely sore in the muscles, but after two more days on the bumpy roads and trails they now had actual skin rashes and Carter even had a blister on the inside of one of his thighs. It was exceedingly painful for both of them and when they got back to their hotel room they could barely walk.

Each of them was extremely cast down. They had not found Caleb, their butts and legs were sensitive to the touch, and on top of it all, when they had dropped the quads back at the base camp the machines were immediately loaded onto the trailers that they were brought in on; the official search really was being called off. They just couldn't believe it. They hugged and shared tears with Tawna. This was the toughest part of the job for her. Calling off a search when the lost person was yet to be found was so difficult, but she couldn't be ruled by emotions. She had to be sensible about how and where the resources at her disposal were used.

Back at the hotel Carter and Layla hoped showering off and getting clean would help relieve some of the pain from the sores on their bodies. When the warm water hit the raw flesh on their backsides and the backs of their legs it was like being poked with thousands of red hot needles, all at the same time. They needed to cleanse their skin though, so they gritted their teeth and soaped up and cleaned their wounds as best they could.

After drying off and putting Vaseline on their skin sores, they dressed for bed and lay down. Not a word had been spoken since they had gotten to their room. They were both resting on the bed next to each other, Layla under the covers and Carter lying on top of them. Lying there they each stared up at the ceiling that was textured with what looked like a layer of cottage cheese, the same kind of texturing they both had in their homes while growing up.

Layla remembered that, as a child, she would stare up from her bed at night and, by the dim light coming from her lamp on the nightstand, she would look for shapes or figures in the texture of the ceiling. She, and many other children she presumed, would do the same thing outside with clouds in the summer, when they were big and fluffy, like giant pieces of cotton hung in the blue sky.

Carter's hand slipped into Layla's and squeezed. Tears escaped from the corners of his eyes and ran down into his ears. Layla followed suit and soon they were curled tightly into each other, sharing silently in their sadness and fears.

DAY 7

The horizon was nothing but a faint glow when Caleb awoke. He tried to move and failed. He was so sore and stiff from sleeping on the ground, in the same position all night, that it seemed like he would never be able to move again. When he did manage to shift his posture, it was so slow and painful that he contemplated just lying there forever, perfectly still. Obviously, that was not an option. He was tired, hungry, thirsty, and, oh yeah, he had a *knife stuck in his right thigh!*

He lay there, contemplating this setback to any survival plans he may have had. The good thing was that his wound hadn't bled so much that he had died of blood loss. He was still alive...bonus! Still, he knew that he would need to remove the knife and that scared him. His immediate concern was how bad it was going to hurt and also that it might cause him to bleed again, maybe fatally this time.

Caleb decided he needed to sit up. It took him about ten minutes in all. He managed to roll over onto his side and raise himself to his left elbow. He then extended his arm and propped himself up into a sitting position. By the time he made it upright, he was exhausted and out of breath. Peering down at the knife handle he could now see clearly, since the sun had risen more and was just about to break the horizon, a large, dark black stain on his pant leg. In movies and television shows blood is bright red and dramatic, but he realized that wasn't the case at all. Maybe it was vibrant red when a person was in the act of bleeding, like the time he had cut his finger with an extremely sharp chef's knife while helping to chop vegetables for dinner. In that situation, the liquid was indeed very red, but now he remembered that a couple of days later, when he removed the bandage that his mother had put on his finger, that the dried blood was a very dark brown, almost black. Looking at his leg now it looked to be the same.

As the area around him continued to brighten with the rising sun he took in his surroundings. Splayed out in front of him were the remnants of his ladder. It had worked just fine when he was climbing straight up and when he was standing relatively still. When he had started moving more frantically, though, after being stung and leaning over too far, the lashings he had tightened multiple times gave out; they turned out to not be tight enough. It was still loosely kept together by the boot laces and belt, etc., but it looked like it had been picked up by a giant of a man and then thrown right back down onto the earth.

While surveying the area he noticed something else that he hadn't seen at first. There were depressions in the dirt surrounding the ladder. He squinted his good eye to try and get a more focused look at the depression and, when he fully realized what it was he was looking at, his heart stopped and his stomach turned sour. Ignoring temporarily the stiffness in his body and the pain that it caused, he hurriedly scooted backwards on his butt using both arms and his one good leg, dragging the wounded one along, until his back was snug up against a large tree opposite the one with the beehive. He looked around hysterically with his good eye wide open, searching...for a bear. He saw none at the moment and returned his eye and his thoughts to the area underneath the hive. Or, he realized, where the beehive *used* to be.

Holy crap! The hive is GONE! Caleb's heart continued to beat exceedingly fast because of his fear and he looked around quickly as he tried to slow his breathing so that he could listen better. He heard nothing but small chirping sounds calling from one tiny bird to another. They were probably saying "good morning" to each other, completely unaware that below them a boy not yet old enough to drive a car was severely injured and scared for his life.

Caleb again assessed the situation. He saw that there were claw marks on the tree trunk, but his instinct told him that they weren't impressions left by the bear for marking territory. They weren't super deep, nor were they all one on top of the other. Knowing that the hive was gone, and how high up it had been, he came to the conclusion that the marks were from when the bear climbed the tree and knocked the beehive down. All this while Caleb lay on the ground passed out. A cool shiver coursed down his spine at this thought.

He looked closer under the branch and around the jumbled ladder and saw pieces of the torn apart hive, it didn't appear that the animal had left any honey behind at all.

So the bear wasn't tall enough to get the beehive without standing up on its hind legs? That's good. Still, it's a freakin' bear! In this area it's probably a black bear. It didn't attack me, even though I was only a few feet away. Maybe it thought I was dead. Or maybe it didn't think I looked very tasty and went for the honey instead. Still, it might come back. I do NOT plan on being here for that.

Caleb's immediate thoughts then returned to the knife in his leg. He needed to remove it and do so quickly. He was afraid a sudden removal might tear open his wound more than necessary, but he also feared that if he went too slow he'd pass out again before it came all the way out. If he passed out one more time he would prefer that the knife had been removed so he wouldn't have to try again when he was revived.

That being decided, he needed something to tie around his leg to promptly stop the bleeding. He didn't want to give up his jacket, but he could give up the sleeves on his TREE REX shirt. They weren't long, but he thought he could rip them off and use them as a bandage to press against the wound. He removed his jacket, followed by his shirt and attempted to tear the sleeves at the seams, he didn't have the strength to do it. He needed the knife to cut them off, but it was still in his leg! Caleb doubled down on his efforts and ultimately got the sleeves to come free.

When that was done, he replaced his now sleeveless shirt and then his jacket. Again he looked around, making certain he remained alone, and then took a few minutes to scoot over to the remnants of his ladder. There he removed his belt from the mess of branches and looped the leather loosely round his leg, just below the knife but above his knee. He slipped sideways and placed his back against the tree trunk, just a few feet below the bear's claw marks.

He took some deep, calming breaths, as he was not quite ready to take the next step. He was motivated by the fear that the bear might return, and he knew that he wouldn't be able to evade attack with a piece of metal buried in his thigh. In addition, the knife was his best—and only—weapon should he need to defend himself. He had to remove it for multiple reasons. Caleb slowly wrapped his fingers around the handle of the knife and took several more deep breaths.

You can do this. You can do this. You NEED to do this. Even with no bear around, you NEED to do this. It's going to hurt, but it's for the best. You NEED to do this.

After giving himself that little pep talk he took three more quick breaths and yanked upward with all his might. A primal scream filled the forest all around him. Birds fled their branches and nests in startled alarm, squirrels scurried for their dens, and insects fell silent, all assessing this new occurrence in the wild. After the slight echo of his yell faded, it was replaced by an eerie, still silence.

The knife dropped from his hand, kicking up little flecks of the soft earth beside him as it landed. Caleb turned his face to the sky. In his eyes he saw shooting stars flickering in and out of his vision and he witnessed a kaleidoscope of colors that gradually faded to black. After yelling every last gasp from his lungs, he sucked in a new, oxygen rich breath and his sight returned.

The pain was so intense that he had no way of describing it with words. His whole body was rigid and shaking in agony, but he was still conscious. A minute—but what felt like ten minutes—after removing the knife he remembered that he needed to bandage the stab wound. He brought his chin down and saw blood slowly oozing from his leg. Again, he became lightheaded and had to concentrate on his breathing. It was crucial that he stop the blood flow as he couldn't afford to pass out.

He focused all his energy on placing the

shirtsleeves he had ripped off his t-shirt, stacking one on top of the other, each folded in half, onto the wound. They were just large enough to cover the cut and he pressed down on them with his hand, wincing at the same time. Holding them in place with his right hand he used his left to reach down and slide the belt farther up his leg until it was over the bandage. When it was in place, he tightened it and then fell back against the tree in exhaustion.

•••••

At the same time that all this was happening Carter and Layla were sitting next to each other fully dressed on the edge of their unmade bed. Since they woke up, they had been talking about the next logical step. They concluded that it was a good idea for her to return home and be with Amber. This whole situation was difficult on the entire family, not just them. She had been staying with friends from church who had kids of the same age as her. Both Layla and Carter knew that she was being well taken care of, but they thought it important, after being gone for so many days already, to have one of them go back and be with her.

They were sure that Amber would find more comfort at this time with her mother than with Carter. That was the deciding factor when choosing which one of them would go home and which one would stay on to continue the search.

"I'll be sure to contact you as often as possible," Carter said to Layla.

"I know you will," she replied.

"And you need to keep me up to date with how Amber's doing. This has got to be extremely tough on her as well."

"I will, I will," Layla said, trying her best to hold back the tears that were just aching to be let free from her eyes. She agreed with Carter that this was the right decision. Still, she couldn't prevent the feeling that she was abandoning her eldest child who was out in the woods alone going through who knows what. The official search for him had already been called off! How could she do this?

"I just got off the phone with Dougie. He gave me directions to a dirt landing strip not too far away. Apparently it hasn't been used—by anyone he knows about anyway—in a long time. A local told him it should still be serviceable." Carter paused, then continued, wrapping his arm around Layla's rounded shoulders, "I'm going to go out there and check the strip to make sure landing is possible, and then signal him when he arrives whether to actually try it or not. I'm going to go up with him to search some more." Layla nodded her head and raised a hand to wipe away a tear that had broken free. "We're going to find him, babe. We're going to find him."

"We don't know that, Carter," she said with a shaky voice, her gaze focusing on the worn hotel carpet. "It's been seven days, *seven*. That's a long time and he's alone and there are animals out there and he has no food and he might be hurt and..," she trailed off and leaned forward. She brought both hands up to cover her face and sobbed.

"I'm scared too, babe, I'm so scared," he took a deep breath. "I've got to put those fears aside though so I can keep looking. I think maybe you should have a good cry with Amber too, then help her turn it around into being optimistic that we'll find him. He's not gone forever, we're going to find him one way or another." It was just a simple phrase that people say all the time, "one way or another", but in Layla's mind she heard "dead or alive". She sobbed some more. Carter realized his mistake in phrasing and let out a defeated, deflating breath and his shoulders sagged.

"I didn't mean it like that, I mean...we're going to find him, alive," he said, trying to convince himself that it was true. It was very hard at this point to keep up a good attitude. They both sat there for a few minutes, consumed by their private thoughts. Eventually Layla stood up, having gained her composure back.

"You need to get going, you need to make sure that landing strip is good before Dougie shows up. I'll go home to Amber and let her know it's okay to be scared and afraid, and to also keep faith."

Carter stood up and walked with his wife to the doorway and they embraced in a tight hug. After a few seconds they parted, but held on to each other's arms and looked each other in the eye. Never in their wildest dreams did they ever think this would be what life dealt them. They had been married for almost 20 years now and when they first got engaged they knew that their life together would not be all roses and butterflies. There would be tough times, but this, this was something no one could anticipate.

"Go find our son," she said.

"I will."

•••••

A few minutes after cinching the belt down on his leg, Caleb's foot began to tingle. It was the same sensation as when he had sat too long on the sofa at home in a funny position without moving while watching a show or playing video games. His foot would tingle as it "fell asleep" and then when he moved it or stood up it tingled even more, sometimes even felt hot, and often hurt as his foot "woke up".

Once he had asked his mom what that feeling was and she said it was because of the way he had crossed his legs, it was cutting off the blood supply to his foot; the tingling was a sensation produced by his blood not circulating properly. When he changed position and the blood flow was returned it resulted in an increased, intense prickling feeling that was at times painful, then it eventually went away.

That was *exactly* what Caleb was feeling right now, and luckily he had his wits about him enough to realize what it was: he had cinched the belt down on his thigh too tight. The belt had done its job well enough. The bleeding hadn't soaked through the layers of the t-shirt sleeves at all, but now he realized it might be because he had been too aggressive with the tightening. He reached down with the tip of his knife and he cut a new hole in the leather of the belt an inch away from where it currently doubled over on top of the buckle. When that was complete, he made one more an inch above that one, just in case he needed to adjust it again after this first try.

He set the knife down in the dirt and pine needles next to him. He could see a few streaks of shiny metal showing through, but most of its blade was still covered in blood. He retrieved the end of the belt, which he had pulled down tight between his thighs, and tucked it under his injured leg to keep the tension. The belt loosened and he slowly slid the leather down through the clasp of the buckle and put the metal prong through the new hole he had cut.

The relief wasn't immediate, but after two or three minutes the tingling faded. It didn't hurt like it sometimes did when blood flow returned, but he thought about it and realized that that usually happened when he stood up after his foot had fallen asleep. Maybe it had something to do with gravity pulling the fluid back down to his foot quickly. Either way, he felt like it had worked and was relieved that, for the first time since falling, he had completed a task without it resulting in pain.

I really don't want to move, Caleb thought to himself. He knew any sort of movement would be slow and zombie-like in addition to hurting, but he *had* to move. At a minimum he required water and he needed to get to the berry bush and eat the last of those berries. His body lacked nutrition before this incident, but now that he was injured, he would be needing it even more. He also wanted to get away from this location as soon as possible because the bear might return at any time. His need to get up and move served two needs: get some food, evade the bear.

Before moving he wiped the blade of his knife on a part of his pants that didn't have any blood on it and then replaced it in its sheath. He used his three good limbs to scoot towards what remained of the ladder where he untied and pocketed the waist strap that had been used to keep it together. He grabbed the jacket drawstring pieces as well and tied the ends to make one long piece, then threaded it through the belt loops of his pants. His belt was now on his leg and he needed the drawstring to keep his pants up.

He got his boot laces untangled from the mess and brought his left knee up to his chest and reached down to lace up his boot. When that was done, he thought about lacing his right boot, but he knew there was no way that he'd be able to bend his knee to perform the same task. He thought about removing the boot, lacing it up, and then putting it back on, but he honestly didn't know if he could take it off. If taking it off was going to be a problem, then pulling it back on and then trying to tighten the lace would be virtually impossible, so for the moment he pocketed the boot lace in his jacket pocket and zipped it closed. He would have to get around with just one boot on tight.

Speaking of getting around, he hadn't even tried to stand up yet, but with the damage done to his leg he knew that he wouldn't be able to move away from the area without something to help him. He would need to fashion a crutch out of something. He looked back at the leftovers of his ladder. Eyeing one of the longer pieces that was laying there he thought it might be the correct length for a makeshift crutch, but he'd have to stand up to find out for sure.

Caleb reluctantly flipped over from sitting on his backside to being on all fours, but in this case it was "all threes" since his right leg stuck out straight to the side. He walked his hands up the tree trunk and made a very awkward hop/jump move to get up on his feet without bending the leg. He stood there for a minute catching his breath and then realized that the branch he intended to try out was still laying on the ground.

"SON...of...a...*BISCUIT!*" he exclaimed. The last thing he wanted to do was get back down on the ground and then crawl back up the side of the tree to his standing position, but that's exactly what he was going to have to do. He would pick up both of the longer branches to try them out and decide which would serve best.

He went through the whole painful process and, once he was back on his feet, he took off his jacket. Once that was removed, he tried tucking each of the branches under his right armpit and selected the one that was the more appropriate height. Luckily, he wouldn't need to find a taller or shorter one. When he had chosen the serviceable branch, he took the jacket he had removed and wrapped it over and around the top of the new crutch several times. Once that was done, he tucked it snugly up under his arm again and tested it out, it seemed to be just right.

He still needed to secure it in place though. The bootlace he had saved would be perfect, so he unwrapped the jacket, removed the lace from the pocket, re-wrapped the top of the branch with the jacket, and tied it all in place.

With that finished it was time to venture away from his failed attempt to gather honey and he took his first few steps with the crutch. They were very short, very herky-jerky, yet he kept his balance well enough and slowly made progress in the direction of his campsite. It took a bit of time, but once there he was able to bend over, pick up his water bottle, and down the contents. His thirst was immense, but he had put it out of his mind because there were other, more pressing matters to attend to first.

He recapped the bottle and set about gathering up all his items. The sleeping bag and sleeping pad were stuffed into the largest compartment of the backpack and...well, that was it. He didn't have much other than that and what he was wearing. His leg was throbbing just from being upright for these few minute, but he pressed on.

He looked down at the remnants of this shelter, which, since he had removed the jacket drawstring, lay collapsed before him. It was just a bunch of tree limbs, but he had worked hard figuring out how get it to stand up, as well as how to use his knife to remove the pine needle laden branches for the sides of the little dwelling. He stood there a little longer feeling sentimental about leaving his shelter of the last four nights. He needed to move though, so it didn't last long.

It's just a shelter. It's not even a living thing, he reasoned with himself. Why was he getting all choked up over this? *I'm just tired and afraid to head back out into the unknown, I guess.*

He managed his pack onto his back and clicked the chest strap together. He moved over to the stream and, with the assistance of the crutch, lowered himself to the ground and refilled his water bottle, drank some more, and topped it off again. The bottle was replaced in the side pocket of the pack that he could access without having to take it completely off. He turned on the heel of his left boot and headed off to the berry bush.

In the back of his mind Caleb had been mildly worried that the bear might have passed by the berry bush after demolishing the beehive and eaten all the berries too, but when he arrived he saw that the branches still had plenty on them. He hadn't had anything to eat in almost 24 hours now and he was extremely hungry. He stood there and instead of collecting them in his hat, like he had previously, he just popped them into his mouth just as quickly as he could pick them.

Ten or so minutes later he had picked the bush clean. He even ate all of the fruit that wasn't quite ripe yet, but still edible. There were no more berries to be had and Caleb's stomach was full for the first time in a long time. He didn't ration the food out on this visit, since he knew he was not coming back. There was no sense in leaving any of the fruit behind, he might as well gorge himself. He removed his bottle and sipped, not drinking too much water as his belly was already on that edge between full and overly full.

The container was replaced in his pack, the berry bush was berry-less now, and it was time to move on. He had decided that he would continue to follow the water, he wasn't willing to leave that. Unfortunately, he was leaving the big X he had spent so much time and energy making, but he wasn't even sure people would still be looking for him, let alone from the air. He had only heard, he thought, a helicopter that one time, and that seemed like an eternity ago.

Trudging through his camp one final time he looked around. He made sure he hadn't accidentally dropped or forgotten to pack something that he would be wanting. Patting the knife in its sheath to verify he still had it with him he was satisfied that he had it all and he started on his way.

Hours on into his trek he paused to take a break. After resting for a few moments, it went from being a short break to staying for the night. He had wanted to stop many times before he actually did, but he needed to get as much distance from the bear tracks as possible. He at long last stopped because his injured leg was *killing* him. It hurt so bad that he had no way of truly describing the pain he was in. Also, on top of having the stab wound, the underside of his right arm was slowly bruising and forming a rash from the rubbing of the makeshift crutch.

When he was 5 or 6 years old, Caleb had broken his foot. He was out in the street on his bike doing "tricks" while at the same time shooting a foam dart gun. Carter and Layla didn't quite understand how exactly something like that was possible, but that was the story Caleb gave them. In the end, one of Caleb's dart-gun battle-bike "tricks" went wrong and he lost his balance, tipping over and trapping his foot under the frame of the bike while the rest of his body came down on top of that. The result was a broken foot and a couple months of using crutches to get around. Those crutches were factory made out of aluminum tubing with cushy foam pads on top. They were as comfortable as crutches could be, yet they still caused bruising and chafing after extended use. One can imagine how much worse his homemade crutch was.

What I wouldn't give to have those nice crutches right now.

The crutch he was using, while serviceable, was causing problems and he had to pause more than once during the day to untie, re-wrap the jacket/padding, and then retie it in order to make it as comfortable as possible. Despite all that, it was still a tree branch with a jacket wrapped around one end, not the most ideal. Unfortunately, he didn't have any other real options to make it more comfortable or anything to keep it from chafing his skin. It was what it was.

So, when Caleb stopped it was a relief not just for his leg, but also for his underarm and the side of his torso. Thankfully, he had water at his disposal and, up to that point anyway, the weather had been working in his favor. He wasn't worried too much about sleeping without a shelter right now. He hadn't seen any berry bushes during his trek that day, and he had been actively watching out for them. He did, though, manage to find a little bit of food earlier.

Berries were what he had looked for, but weren't the only thing he was willing to eat. Unfortunately, in his current state he wasn't going to be able to catch any squirrels or rabbits, so that was out. He had, however, needed to walk around a fallen tree earlier in his hike and something caught his eye.

Under normal circumstances he would have climbed over the tree and jumped down to the other side, but that wasn't an option. He wished that he could've just hopped over it instead of walking around the 75 foot long timber, but that was the only play he had.

The detour around the tree turned out to be a blessing in disguise. When Caleb came to the end of the tree its roots were sticking out of the ground that had left a good sized crater in the earth. He looked at the root system and saw what looked like little off-white bugs moving around. When he looked closer, he realized that he knew what they were: they were grubs!

"Oh, gross!" Caleb had exclaimed and wrinkled up his nose in disgust. He was about to move on, when he remembered a previous camping trip that he had taken with the scouts. Mr. Holman had pointed out to the boys some grubs that he had spotted on a fallen log.

Boys, see those little white, wormy looking things? Those are grubs. I think they are larvae of a beetle judging by the size of them. Kind of like how a butterfly is a caterpillar before it turns into an adult butterfly. These grubs are the youth stage of a beetle before it becomes, well, a beetle.

At that the boys took a closer look at them and were kind of grossed out, but they were about to get even more disgusted, they just didn't know it yet.

Here's the thing boys, Mr. Holman had said, while picking up one of the larva, *if you ever get stuck out in the woods, and are all out of food, you can eat these*. And with that he popped it into his mouth, chewed it, tried really hard not to show how gross it was by maintaining an expressionless face, and then drank some water, opening his mouth and sticking his tongue out to demonstrate that he had eaten it. The boys were so grossed out that they screamed and yelled and ran around yelling about how crazy Mr. Holman was.

For five or so minutes after that event, Mr. Holman had tried to get the scouts to try one, even offering a bribe of a double cheeseburger meal on the way back home from the trip. He got no takers. Caleb, while thinking back on it, couldn't figure out if Mr. Holman was honestly trying to teach them a survival technique, or if he was just being gross. He was good at being gross, that's why the boys loved him. Caleb's parents even talked about how he was just a big kid and how he was the perfect scout leader. He thought about it more and figured that his leader would say, "Who says I wasn't both teaching you *and* being gross?"

Caleb looked at the grubs and, while in the past it was a disgusting thought, didn't think they looked so bad now. Back then, he'd had a choice; he could have eaten a grub or an energy bar. He could have also eaten some beef jerky or trail mix from his bag. Today, though, he didn't have an option, other than eat the grubs or continue to go hungry...with his next meal being very uncertain.

Deciding to try them out and get something in his belly, he leaned his crutch against the large tree trunk and balanced himself with his right hand on the crunchy crust of the bark. With his left hand he reached into one of the crevices between the exposed roots and picked up a grub with his fingertips. He stared at it for a long time, working up the courage to toss it into his mouth. He was hungry, but it was still gross.

Finally, his desire to eat overcame his fear of the unknown and he quickly flung the larva into his open mouth and started chewing. The initial *pop* the bug made as he crushed it between his molars caused him to retch and he almost threw up. The sensation of the pop, a few seconds after the fact even, made him gag again. He swiftly got his water bottle out of his pack and washed the thing down with a big gulp of water. He followed it with another swig and swished it around inside his mouth before spitting the water out onto the ground near his feet.

"Aaaalllgggggphphphlllllllptt, that was SO GROSS!!!" he had yelled to the silent forest, as he drug his forearm across his mouth. "Blaaacht!" he uttered and then shook his head side to side rapidly like a dog shaking water off of its fur, then he got dizzy and almost fell over. Falling over would *not* have been good at all, but he set the bottle down on the top of the tree trunk and steadied himself with both hands.

"Okay, that was gross, but you can do this," he stated to himself. He tried to wipe the vision of the grubs as slimy bugs from his mind. He tried to think of them as if they were nothing but calories. Calories were of ultimate importance, he needed to get calories into his system for the energy he'd need to heal and to keep moving.

He picked up his water bottle and grabbed another grub. With the second grub he took a different tactic and tried popping it like a pill. He opened his mouth, tossed the grub in, took a swig of water, and swallowed it whole. This was much less disgusting than the first try so he repeated it over and over. He ate his fill of grubs, but knew his fullness was also in part due to all the water he had drunk washing down the small bugs.

That brought him to where he was at right now, sitting on a fallen tree farther downstream. He'd been moving all day and it had been a *long* day. It was hard to believe that about 24 hours earlier he had been standing on top of his ladder getting ready to feast on honey. It was just this morning that he pulled a knife from his leg and then freaked out because he was surrounded by bear tracks.

He sat on the log in a trance, staring at the ground without focusing on it, while thinking about everything that had happened. If someone had seen him at that moment, they probably would have described what appeared to be a young boy in his early teens who was bloody and dirty all over, his clothes ripped and torn. He was sitting so still that this unknown observer in the woods might even think it was some sort of statue out in the middle of the forest, possibly giving it the title of "The Survivor". He was the perfect picture of surviving at this exact moment. He didn't know it, he didn't see it, but he was living it and doing it! He was surviving, no matter what setbacks had come his way.

Caleb eventually stopped zoning out and got up enough mental energy to decide what needed to happen next. He wanted to find more food, but, more importantly, he felt his body required a rest. He slowly let himself down to the ground right where he was. He unrolled his sleeping pad and scooted over on top of it, then pulled his bag out of his pack. He unzipped the zipper all the way so that he could use it as a blanket because he didn't think he could slide into the bag in the same manner he would normally use because of his injured leg. He grabbed his crutch and laid it down near his head, using the padded end of it as a hard, but serviceable pillow.

As he was arranging the crutch/pillow he said a small prayer in his heart.

Lord, please help me to heal, please help my parents to not lose faith in their search.

He had barely formed the words of his appeal in his mind before he was fast asleep, his body drinking in the rest like a dehydrated person would water. In his deep sleep he dreamed vividly of two things: he dreamt of his parents being the ones to find him out here in the wild and the other was of the most creamy, delicious, HUGE bowl of chicken fettuccine alfredo with mushrooms, peas, and bacon bits topped off with an abnormally large helping of freshly shredded Parmigiano-Reggiano cheese.

•••••

Dougie and Carter stood next to Dougie's single engine Cessna 172 on the airstrip locked in a tight hug. The men had spent all day scanning the forest for Carter's son. After hours of searching in the morning, they had flown one hour to the south to refuel the aircraft, use the bathroom, and get some food and water. Carter didn't tell Dougie at the time, but he also really needed to reapply some ointment to his chapped butt. Sitting in the mildly vibrating plane all day was much nicer than sitting on the seat of a quad, but the injury had already been sustained and still needed some tending.

Even after refueling both their bodies and the plane, they still had no luck in their afternoon search. Hours were spent in the air and eyes became fatigued, but still they had tried. Once the sun had gotten close to the horizon, Dougie said he needed to get Carter back on the ground and then back in the air before losing all of the light. The airstrip was just a dirt and grass covered lane with no lights, so getting in the air soon was important. They gripped each other for a dozen or so seconds and then let go. Dougie was crying, but Carter was dry eyed.

"I'm sorry buddy, I just...I'm so

sorry," Dougie exhaled and rubbed his eyes with the heels of his hands. They could both feel his tiredness and his exasperation. He had been the one that had kept up the energy and optimism of finding the boy. He had also logged 27 hours of flight time over the past two days. Carter hadn't asked, but was sure that some sort of flight rules were being broken by his friend in his efforts. Dougie was mentally, physically, and emotionally exhausted. He couldn't keep his tears in check anymore, particularly because he had felt so confident in them finding Caleb.

"I thought we would find him Carter, I really did. I've flown over this whole area for hours and hours....and nothing," he said, spreading his arms apart, palms up, showing his empty hands.

"I know bud, I know, we did our best," Carter said, and caught himself, "We're *doing* our best." He hoped that his slip wasn't an indicator of losing hope or giving up. It was real that if they didn't find him very soon, they would have to give up the search. It broke his heart to think about it; it caused an actual, physical pain in his chest.

"I gotta get going, man," Dougie said, interrupting Carter's thoughts. "The light's going quick, so I need to get airborne." They embraced one more time and Dougie climbed into the pilot's seat and closed the door. Carter watched his friend as he quickly went through an abbreviated pre-flight instrument and flight controls check. After just a few minutes, the starter kicked the propeller around until the engine caught. He walked over to the side of the airstrip as the aircraft taxied down to the far end of the runway so that when he took off he could do it into the light wind. The plane made the 180 degree turn once it reached the end of the strip and Dougie pushed the throttle all the way forward. He used most of the grassy lane before getting up to the minimum speed for flight and then nosed upwards, taking to the skies. He went airborne right as he passed Carter and gave him a little wave. Carter returned the salute even though Dougie had already gone by him and wouldn't see it.

Carter remained where he was standing for a couple of minutes, his hands stuffed into the pockets of his jeans. He stood there and watched the red and green wingtip lights and the flashing white strobe light of the plane fly off into the distance, its silhouette fading into the darkening night sky. He turned away and walked towards the small four door rental car he had driven out just this morning. As he approached the car he noticed that one of the hubcaps was missing. He knew for a fact that it was not missing when he and Layla had picked up the car.

"Dammit!" he yelled and kicked the tire of the wheel lacking the hubcap. He turned his face up to the few twinkling stars and, raising his arms up and facing skyward, he wailed to the heavens.

"What else are You going to do to us?! We've prayed and been faithful! For what? We, along with hundreds of others, have helped search for Caleb and we've received nothing but heartache to show for it! I've shown my faith by appealing for Your mercy and pleaded for Your intervening hand. We've shown our faith in action by being out there, trying to be the tool by which we are able to find our son!" Caleb dropped his arms so they hung limply by his sides. His face went from anger to complete sadness and he lowered his chin all the way down until it rested on the collar of his flannel shirt.

"What else are You going to do to us?" he asked again, but instead of yelling he now asked it in a quiet voice. He stared at the wheel on the car. He could see the places around the edge of the black steel rim where it had prevented dirt from dirtying the wheel before it got knocked off. He eventually stopped staring and moved over to the car, pulled up on the handle of the door to open it, and sat down in the driver's seat.

After closing the door, he pulled the seatbelt across his chest and clicked it into place. He removed the key from his jacket pocket. Instead of inserting it into the ignition switch he just sat there with his hands in his lap, key at the ready in his right hand, and stared out at the darkness through the windshield.

Before he realized it, he was in a deep sleep with his head tilted back against the headrest and his mouth hung open. He even had a small bit of drool making its way down the side of his chin through the stubble of his unshaven face.

DAY 8

Caleb woke feeling like a mummy. Not that he thought he had been carefully wrapped in cloth strips and left in a tomb, he just imagined that a mummy, should it suddenly return to life, would not be able to move very well after having lain in the same position for years. That was exactly how he felt at this moment: cold, stiff, unable to bend at the joints.

He opened his eyes and followed the trunks of the trees up skyward. The pale blue morning sky was just breaking through. He thought about moving his head but it seemed stuck in place. He couldn't even lift his hand. Was he paralyzed? He wiggled his fingers and toes. Nope, good to go. The problem was that his muscles didn't *want* to move.

Lying in the chilly air all night without moving meant it was going to take some serious willpower to get going. On top of that, his right leg was completely stiff. After almost ten minutes of mustering the desire to move, he managed his way up to a sitting position. His stomach was clenched into the tightest knot ever known to mankind; he was so hungry. His dream of delicious Italian food, while wonderful in his sleep, was torturing him now that he was awake.

Caleb had nothing to eat, but he still had water in his bottle. He finished off what was left in the container and it actually made his stomach hurt even more. It was like his stomach was saying, "I want FOOD you idiot, not water, FOOOOOOOOOD!"

"Shut up, I don't have food," Caleb replied to his belly. He leaned over, his hand resting on top of the water bottle, and positioned himself on his knee, then rose up to his good foot. Having learned from the day before, he had prepositioned the crutch against the large log and he grabbed it and tucked it under his arm.

"Ayyye," he moaned with an exaggerated exhale of breath. The underside of his arm now felt like someone had been punching it over and over again. It was extremely tender to the touch. It reminded him of when he had shot his grandpa's shotgun last summer. Even with a pad between the butt of the shotgun and his shoulder, his flesh was bruised and very sensitive from the shotgun's kick for a few days afterwards. He had no way around the pain though, he had to have the support of the crutch to get around.

He moved a few yards away from his sleeping mat and filled his water bottle at the stream. The body of water had become smaller as he had followed it yesterday. It was still flowing well enough, though, to easily fill the container without getting dirt and grit in it.

Over the course of the next half hour he methodically packed up his belongings and got ready to move out. In the morning light he noticed a small patch of clovers tucked under a log not far from where his head had rested. His need for food was so great he thought he'd give them a try. He was fairly sure it wasn't poisonous, so he just went for it. He pinched up patches with his fingertips as he bent over at the waist, using the crutch in his other hand to maintain his balance. He'd stuff the clover into his mouth and chew. It was not very good, but after the grubs he knew he could eat anything. He felt like a cow, chewing the same thing over and over. Eventually each batch would sooner or later be broken down enough to be swallowed with the help of some water.

Don't cows have, like, three or four stomachs or something like that? his mind wandered/wondered. *Man, that's weird.*

He wasn't sure if there was any nutritional value

to the plant, for now he was just happy that it helped to relieve the devastating hunger pangs he had been experiencing.

Once the boy had finished eating, he made one last stop at the water to top off the bottle and headed out. He followed the stream, again keeping an eye out for food and, of course, any evidence of bears. He spent a lot of his time trying to figure out what his best move was. Should he look for another place to settle down? Should he keep moving and hope to come across civilization? Would it be better for his leg injury to rest it or was it beneficial to keep using it? There were so many uncertainties in this whole adventure he was going through.

For the moment, though, he continued travelling, wanting to put more distance between himself and the bear. He might be heading into another type of danger, but he knew for a fact that a dangerous animal was behind him. So, he kept marching on, slowly but consistently.

•••••

Carter awoke in his rental car, stiff from sleeping at night in an awkward position and cold from the cool morning air. Sleeping in the seat of a compact car wasn't ideal. It took a minute or two to fully come out of his sleep, and he started the engine. After a U-turn in the grass he headed back to the road.

As he hit the pavement, he remembered his deep dreams, dreams that weren't vague at all. They were very vivid and easy to remember as he woke up with the sun coming in through the windshield. He recalled that in one dream he and Layla, while out hiking, ran into Caleb. They were looking for him, although they weren't expecting to find him, but suddenly there he was. His son was dirty and skinny, and his clothes were nothing but rags; still, they had found him. Despite his ragged appearance, his mother held a giant bowl of steaming fettuccine alfredo with chicken, bacon, peas, and mushrooms out to him. It looked and smelled absolutely divine. It seemed so tangible in his memory that the vision caused his empty stomach to growl.

As he reviewed the dream in his head, and unknown to his not quite fully alert mind, he had turned onto the road in the opposite direction that he needed to go in order to return to the search area. He was still foggy in the head and it was about 30 minutes of driving before he realized that none of the signs or landmarks along the roadside were familiar.

I should have made it back to the hotel 10 minutes ago, what is going on? he thought to himself, as he looked around to see if he could find anything that he might recognize. It didn't take much time for him to conclude that he was not going the right way. He thought about it for a moment and he realized what he had done.

He pulled over at the next highway pullout to switch directions, but paused when he saw an unmarked trailhead and a trail fading into the forest. It appeared a little bit overgrown and not used much. He sat in the car for a few moments staring at the trail with the engine idling, the exhaust on the vehicle making a very soft purring noise. A minute later he had parked the car closer to the edge of the pavement pullout, exited the vehicle, and locked the car with the remote.

As he tucked away the car key in his pocket, he noticed his reflection in the car window. He saw a man in his mid-forties with hair that was messed up and a face that had three days' worth of dark stubble on his cheeks and chin. He could see that his eyes were sunken from the lack of sleep over the last week; his whole face looked gaunt. The stress he was carrying, the worry of a parent for their child, weighs heavily.

He zipped up his lightweight outdoor jacket a couple more inches, up to his neck, and turned and started down along the trail. He didn't have much of anything with him and this probably wasn't very smart of him. He did, however, have a large bottle of water, one he had purchased when he last filled the car up at the gas station, in the back seat of the car. He didn't have anything to eat, since he hadn't planned on staying out and sleeping in the car, but he had some gum and he just chewed away on that.

Two minutes of hiking down the trail later and he

had disappeared from view of anyone passing by on the highway. The air in the forested shade was cool and had a damp smell to it. He loved that scent, it was one of the things that he adored most about hiking and camping, all the fresh, earthy smells of nature. He was glad that he could still find joy in the moment, despite the circumstances. He continued following the path and waited to see where it would take him.

•••••

Caleb had been up and moving for about an hour when fatigue hit him—and it hit him hard. Being tired and weak had, at this point, become something that he was so used to that he just didn't notice it anymore. It was currently just his lot in life to have no energy and to be in pain, so he had become, to a certain degree, numb to it.

In this instance, however, he was marching along in a zombie-like trance. The next thing he knew, he was so sapped of energy that he almost fell over before he could jerkily lower himself to the ground; he was virtually paralyzed. He thought he had been paying attention and on the lookout for food or traces of bears passing through. In reality, he was zoning out and it was taking all his strength to keep his feet under him and make continued progress along the bank of the flowing water.

As he lowered himself to the ground, his legs and arms shook and he had shivers coursing up and down his back. The clover he had eaten just an hour ago had been good for taking away some of the hunger pangs in his belly, but in reality it did not give any real energy to his depleted body. His body was hitting some sort of invisible wall and right now and it felt like he might not ever be able to get up off the ground again.

Welp, I hope this is a nice place to sit down, because this just might be where I die, he told himself, with a slight smirk on his lips. Making little jokes was something he had been doing the whole morning in order to keep things light, so as to avoid going down the dark path of negative thoughts. This time, however, what he thought really hit him. He thought about dying in a joking tone, but suddenly it became a very real option.

Am I going to die out here? The thought ran circles in his mind. It was the first time he had opened the mental door that let in the possibility that he might not get out of this. It was not a comforting thought. At the same time, it didn't bring along with it the fear that he might have once associated with dying.

I've been a good kid. I'm not perfect, I haven't always been respectful to my parents or nice to Amber, but I'm a good kid. I always tried to be kind to everyone at school, even the kids that others picked on. I wasn't really a good friend to them, but I went out of my way to be kinder.

His mind wandered for a time. It went back to

some of the moments in his life that would always cause him to feel like there was a ball of lead forming in his stomach. Like the time that he called his sister stupid and wouldn't stop treating her like she was mentally challenged in front of his friends, all of it just to try and look cool. He had relentlessly piled on to Amber until she burst into tears and ran to her room. That night she wouldn't come out for dinner and her parents had to go in and ask her what was wrong, but she never told them. Caleb felt sick every time he thought back to that.

Why did I do that? Why did I never apologize? Amber is a great sister, I love her. I don't know why I treated her like that. It probably didn't even make my friends think I was "cool".

Caleb thought of a few other instances where he had acted in a way that wasn't very admirable, then he switched his focus to the good things he had done.

When my mom was really sad after baby Amber was born and she cried a lot, I would help my dad make dinners. We would clean the house, even though I was so young I don't think that I helped very much. I do, however, remember doing it and feeling like it was helping my mom. It was work for me, but I didn't care, because it was going to make her happy.

Caleb paused and reflected on the cheerful memory for a minute or so before moving on to the next pleasant thought.

There was also that time that Tina, from my second grade class with Mrs. Phelps, brought her brand new lunch box to school. There was a colorful cartoon unicorn on it and a glittering rainbow behind it. She was so excited to have it for the beginning of the new school year. Unfortunately, while she was at recess some jerky kids kicked it around like a soccer ball, until it busted open and her lunch flew out all over the school yard. One of the boys stomped on a pudding cup that had fallen on the asphalt and launched chocolate pudding across the four-square court.

Tina was devastated when she saw the mangled box and bawled her eyes out. The boys got in trouble, but Tina was still heartbroken. I don't think her parents had much money, and they couldn't afford to buy her another lunchbox, so she showed up the rest of the week with her food in brown paper lunch bags. I felt so bad for her that I used my allowance and, with the help of some additional money from my mom and dad, went to the store and bought her a new one. I barely knew her, but I wanted to help her feel better. Doing that for another person was probably the best feeling I've had in my whole life.

He thought of those things and a few others. Again, he hadn't been perfect, but he had done many good things in his short life. Was his chance to do more good things in life over? Was this where he died? At the moment, he truly felt like he didn't even have the energy to roll off of his pack that was awkwardly placed between his back and the ground.

I'm a turtle stuck on its back. I can't move. Wiggle, wiggle. He laughed, a light and wheezy laugh.

He lay staring up and one minute rolled into another, then another. His body just didn't have the ability to think and move and heal all at once without eating anything. The human body is very resilient and can take a beating. It can survive for weeks without food, but in this case Caleb was a young, skinny boy. He didn't have very much in fat reserves for his body to use as energy while he was running out of food. In addition to that, while already having proven himself mentally tough and able to get through difficult situations, it was physically draining to be alert at all times in a survival situation. He had only had a few instances throughout this whole chain of events where he had completely shut off his brain and rested fully.

Most impactful of all, though, was the injury the knife had done to his thigh when he had fallen from the ladder under the beehive. The body has amazing self-healing capabilities, particularly in younger people like Caleb. Healing, though, requires energy and his body just didn't have any food or fat to pull that energy from. There's a reason people go to the hospital to get care. Of course, they see a doctor and that's a huge factor, but they also get plenty of healthy foods and rest to promote healing. Caleb had none of those things and it had exhausted him. It seemed he had reached the limits of his capabilities. In addition, his injury more than likely wasn't mending properly, or as quickly as it could.

He thought more about the wound healing properly. Since loosening the belt one notch to relieve the tingling in his foot, he hadn't messed with it at all. He thought about it and concluded that he really ought to check the cut, he just needed to muster the strength to do so. He hadn't cleaned the gash and there was probably dirt and honey and who knows what else in there. He didn't have any rubbing alcohol or anything that would disinfect the wound, but he could at least try flushing it with water. Also, he realized as he thought about it more, he needed to change out the bandage for a clean one. An infection at this point could be deadly.

With the new mini-mission of caring for his leg, Caleb was able to dig deep and muscle his way up to a sitting position.

I am NOT going to die today. Not today. Let's do this!

It was a process that in everyday life would have only lasted about 15 seconds. Today, though, was not in any way a normal day and it took him almost four minutes to remove his backpack. After that, he sat there for another five, gathering his strength to keep moving. While resting he pondered on what he could use as a clean bandage. He had nothing useful in his pack and the pack itself was made out of material that would not soak up any blood or pus coming from the cut. He thought about the shirt he had on, but he couldn't walk around with no shirt on and he couldn't start wearing the jacket because he needed that as the padding on the top of the crutch.

He contemplated cutting off his right pant leg below the knee, he could live without that. Unfortunately, his pants were definitely the dirtiest thing he had on. Everything was dirty in fact, but the pants were fairly disgusting. Using that as a bandage might do more harm than good if he switched out the current t-shirt bandage with the nasty pants fabric.

Well, I need to switch it out, so I guess it has to be the t-shirt.

Caleb slowly and with some difficulty removed his shirt. Using his knife, he cut off the bottom six inches of the garment. After replacing the knife in its sheath, he put what remained of his shirt back on. He gave a little, weak laugh as he looked at his outfit. He was now wearing a sleeveless t-shirt that stopped just above his belly button.

I look like a wannabe surfer, Caleb thought. *I look ridiculous.*

Looks were definitely not of any true importance right now, though, so he carried on. He turned the recently cut loop of shirt over in his hands to try and find what looked like the cleanest part. When he found the spot that he thought was the least dirty, he folded the cloth in half twice, with the "clean" portion on the bottom. With that ready, he painfully twisted around to get his water from the pocket of his backpack.

Caleb realized as he did this that he hadn't had a drink in a long time and figured that that was not helping anything at all. He took several large gulps after he got his hands on the bottle, but didn't drink it all. He set the container down, lid still off, and started to undo the buckle on the belt. The pain was immediate and sharp. He winced and got lightheaded, but kept working. He undid the belt and looked at the t-shirt bandage, it was almost completely soaked in his dark, dried blood.

He tried to peel up the cloth to reveal the injury, but the dried blood acted like a glue, keeping the bandage stuck to his leg.

Great, yet another dilemma. Can I just get one simple, straightforward task here?

He wasn't sure if he should keep removing it and risk ripping the wound open again, or if he should just leave it. His leg hurt so bad when he touched it.

That's because it is probably infected, bud. It was the voice of Mr. Holman again. Caleb knew it was his own mind creating this imaginary commentary, but it was still extremely comforting to have it. *If it's that tender, then I don't think I need to tell you that that's the case. When a wound becomes infected it becomes swollen and extremely red and painful to the touch, that's you pal.*

Caleb knew all this from scout training, but hadn't really thought all that deeply about it because at this point in his life just thinking was tiring.

Don't worry about it Caleb, I'll help you through it. I know it's going to hurt really bad and seem like a terrible idea in the moment, but you have to get that dirty bandage off your leg.

Caleb peeled back the corner of the t-shirt material and it began hurting all over again.

Just do it. Don't rip too hard, but don't go slowly either. Be deliberate with your action. You've got your water and a new bandage ready, just make it happen.

"Make It Happen", that was a phrase that Mr. Holman always said to the boys. He was a man that always told the boys to formulate a plan and then take action on it.

"Okay, let's make it happen," Caleb said in a dry, raspy voice that was barely audible. He once again started pulling back on the corner of the bandage, but this time, despite the shooting pain, he pulled it all of the way off at a moderate pace, trying to avoid ripping off more of the scabbing than necessary. With the final tug it came free in his hand and he fell back, shocked by the agony this action had caused. As he lay there for a moment, his eyes saw twinkling pinpoints of light that came and went as well as transparent clouds of color. He had heard of people "seeing stars" when in great pain, or after hitting their head, but the hazy colors were something he had never heard of.

He urged his body to sit up again, bending at the waist. The wound still needed to be cleaned and the clean bandage applied. He assessed the gash peeking out from the cut in his pant leg. Removing the bandage had caused the wound to start bleeding again, but nothing that was overly concerning. Grabbing his knife, he made the hole in his pants larger so he could get a better look at his leg.

He immediately determined the cut to be infected, just like he had suspected it might be. It was swollen and tender, and not just because he had ripped off the scab only moments ago. Yellowish/brown liquid was oozing out of the deep wound, as well as it had soaked into the bandage he had removed. Caleb grabbed the discarded bandage and used the corners, the only parts of the fabric that hadn't soaked up any of the pus or blood, to wipe away as much of the gross looking fluid as possible. It looked very much like the greenish-yellow snot of a sick child...so disgusting.

He inhaled sharply through his gritted teeth and winced in pain as he ran the cloth over the exposed flesh.

He picked up his water bottle and dumped the remainder of its contents onto the wound, trying to wash away as much pus, blood, and dirt as he could.

There was one last clean corner of the bandage left and he used that to make a final swipe over the wound. He then picked up the new bandage and set it gently over the gash. The belt was run back through the buckle and he tightened it back down to the notch that it had been in previously. The leg had slightly swelled up since he had released the belt and it ached fiercely as he cinched the belt back down, but he thought it important to keep it on there tight.

The procedure was complete and again he laid back to rest his weary body. The whole thing had completely worn him out all over again and the thought of never being able to get up again once more began to run through his mind. This thought was counterproductive, but he had learned out here in the wilderness that maintaining a positive attitude and keeping the negative thoughts at a distance takes more energy than he ever would have thought. Still, he tried to push the thoughts away, but at this point he couldn't try as hard as he had before. He thought that maybe it was not such a bad idea to start thinking about dying. Maybe death wouldn't be so horrible if he didn't fight it when it came.

It was while he was thinking those thoughts, and again remembering things he wished he had done differently or been proud of, that he drifted off.

•••••

Carter had started down the trail thirty minutes ago and he was about ready to turn around. The sun wasn't very high yet, but he had been hiking hard and had removed his jacket a few minutes ago, tying it around his waist. He paused in the middle of the path which, surprisingly, was still well worn and easy to follow. Apparently this trail, though not marked by a sign at the highway pull out, was used plenty. It was probably on hiking maps and known among people who go on treks regularly.

He slowly spun around a full 360 degrees in the middle of the footpath while looking off into the woods as far as the trees and bushes would allow. He absentmindedly rubbed his stubbly chin with his right hand. Carter wasn't sure what he was looking for, but he was taking it all in and using that information to decide whether to keep going or to head back. Most of his water was now gone, but he still had a little left in the bottle.

After standing still a minute or so, he began retracing his steps, moving back in the direction of his rental car on the side of the highway. He was looking down at the trail while walking when he felt like something was tugging him from behind, slowing his progress. He turned around and looked down, expecting to see that he had caught the jacket hanging from his waist on a bush, but when he turned around, he saw that it wasn't hung up on anything.

He turned again and started moving back down the path when again he felt the pulling sensation. This time he paid more attention to it. It wasn't an actual physical tugging, but it was more like his body was being urged to not continue back to the car. He stopped, put his hands on his hips, and exhaled.

Man, what is going on here? Am I having a heart attack or a nervous breakdown? Am I feeling weird from having not eaten? Is my stress from this whole thing catching up to me, causing strange body sense issues? What is this?!

Carter looked up and closed his eyes. He breathed deeply through his nose for 30 seconds and pondered what was happening. He was a man who believed in God and maybe he was being guided by His hand. Carter had cursed in anger, in frustration, last night, so why would God still be trying to help him? He knew the answer.

Because God, like any parent, loves his children, even when the children are not showing the gratitude that they ought to. Even when they act like brats all day long, in the moment of their need the parent will always be there for them. Sometimes the parent sits back and lets them go through trials by themselves, but that doesn't mean they've been abandoned, they've just been given room to learn and grow.

Caleb lowered his head and prayed out loud.

"Lord, I'm sorry for my lack of love last night, I ask for Your grace. I don't know if this urging I'm sensing in my body is from You or not, but I'm going to follow it. I ask You to please direct me to where I need to be."

He opened his eyes and lifted his chin. He wiped at the tears that had gathered at the bottoms of his reddened eyes, then turned away from the highway and ventured farther down the path.

•••••

Caleb was lying on his back. How long he had slept, he did not know. He thought about opening his eyes, it was easier just to leave them closed though. His leg still hurt, but at least he didn't feel his heartbeat pulsing through it anymore, which had been the case right after he had tightened the belt. His mouth was dry, something he wasn't used to since he had had easy access to water the whole time he'd been out here surviving. He had drained his bottle cleaning the wound and had not yet refilled it. He didn't want to get up and get water, nor did he think he had the power to do so even if he did. He was thirsty, oh well.

He continued to lay there, somewhere between sleep and wakefulness for quite some time. The birds in the trees above him sang out, calling from one branch to another. There was a knocking sound echoing about, which he imagined to be a woodpecker out there, just living its life. Every once in a while, he'd hear a random pine cone or branch falling down to the soft ground someplace nearby. Even in its quiet stillness, there was a lot going on in the forest.

He heard the crunch of what he thought was a tiny branch being stepped on in the distance, but he couldn't be sure. It must have been nothing since he didn't immediately hear it again. A minute later, though, he heard *did* it again, and he forced his eyes open slightly. He looked from side-to-side with his eyes without moving his head. He saw nothing.

Caleb wasn't sure if something larger than a squirrel was out there moving around or not, but his ears were now on high alert. He let his eyes fall closed and listened more intently. *Snap.* Pause a few moments. *Snap-pap.* Something was definitely nearby, but what?

Oh crap, it's the bear! It tracked me, following my bloody scent, and has just been waiting for me to collapse and not be able to get back up. His heart immediately began to beat faster and adrenaline was now coursing through his bloodstream.

I need to get out of here. Caleb tried to move, but it was like there was a heavy blanket on top of him. *Snap.* He remembered getting his teeth x-rayed at the dentist. Before taking the x-ray, the dental assistant put a lead lined apron over his shoulders, arms, and chest to protect him from radiation, something that could make him extremely sick. He felt like he had a whole blanket of that lead lined material covering him from his toes all the way to the top of his head, preventing any movement.

Well, I guess this is how it's gonna happen. Maybe this will be quicker than starving to death. But, man, it will for sure be more painful. This sucks!

He reflected on this more and his instinct was to protect himself, even though he knew that his weak, damaged body was no match for a hungry bear. *Snap!* He had a self-defense tool though; he still had his knife. The knife that had been a source of great joy, as well as pain throughout this journey. With all the force he could muster he managed to pull the blade from its sheath and grip the handle in his hand. The bottom of the handle rested by his side on the ground, the blade pointed skyward. If the animal came at him, bear or whatever it was, he'd try his best to plunge it deep into its flesh and hope the beast didn't rip his head off anyway.

Snap, SNAP! Whatever it was, it wasn't trying to be quiet and it was getting closer. *SNAP!! Crunch, crunch.* The animal was now close enough that he could hear the footsteps, even when it wasn't snapping twigs underfoot. *It has to be a bear; it sounds too big and heavy to be anything else.* Caleb flexed his fingers and readjusted his grip on his knife and mentally prepared to strike.

He visualized in his mind one final, powerful thrust propelled by the last of the energy he had remaining in his body. *Crunch, snap.* He could hear it breathing, panting. The bear was running towards him. A primal growl filled the air and, right before the animal struck him, he could feel the atmosphere around his body change. He could feel the air shift slightly over his exposed skin and it brought with it a coolness. It seemed like all other sounds in the forest had been muted. The bear was here, it was time to strike.

Caleb's swung his arm up from his side, across his face and above his head, striking out much faster than he thought possible, even compared to when he was healthy and well fed.

Wow, that was quick! It must be my body's instincts for self-preservation taking over. I'm a freaking closet ninja! He had this last thought while his body was in what felt like slow motion, like his thoughts were moving way faster than what was actually happening there on the forest floor.

His blade struck flesh and the bear growled in pain. It wasn't a good stab. He felt like he had sliced the animal, but not hit it flush. He recoiled his arm to strike again, but the paw of the bear knocked the knife out of his hand and it skittered away, bouncing across the forest floor until it rest in a bed of dried pine needles. His sole shot at survival was now gone, taken away.

He felt the beast put its paw on his head and neck, he was about to die. He could feel its hot breath and drool dripping onto his face. He didn't want to look, but something forced him to open his eyes one last time. He cracked them open, expecting to see the wide, toothy jaws of a bear about to rip his face off. Instead, he saw his father's face, raining tears down onto his own.

Holy crap, that was quick. The bear killed me so fast that I didn't even realize it. It didn't hurt at all and now I'm seeing my dad. A smile of pure joy spread across Caleb's face. *I am SO happy that it wasn't painful at all. It sucks, though, that if my body is ever found that my parents will have to deal with the fact that their son was ripped apart by a bear. It was a quick death, though. SO quick! Wow. I wish I could tell people that dying doesn't hurt so bad.*

"Caleb! CALEB!" Carter yelled into the face of his son. A face that was thinner and dirtier than the last time he had seen it. There were flecks of dirt that appeared to be embedded into various parts of his face. In addition, it was evident that Caleb's right eye had suffered a traumatic event and, while his boy looked up at him, didn't open quite as wide as the other.

"Hi dad, I'm sorry I couldn't survive any longer," Caleb croaked in a low, raspy voice.

"Oh, Caleb!!" his dad said, as he cradled his head and kissed his face.

This feels really, like, REAL. Man, death is so weird.

"Caleb, here, drink this, drink," his dad said, and Caleb felt a bottle pressed against his lips and water pouring into his mouth.

Do dead people feel things? Do I even need to drink this? As Caleb thought this, he began to cough, choking on the water. He coughed and coughed, and his father helped him to sit up.

"Dad?"

"Caleb!" his father shouted, and Caleb could *feel* the relief in his father's voice. When his dad loosened his grasp on him, Caleb looked at him and saw there was blood running down his arm from his right shoulder, a fresh cut visible through a slice in his shirt. He had cut his father when he swung out with his knife!

"Am I alive?" Caleb ask quizzically.

"You're alive! YOU ARE ALIVE!!" his father gushed, "And I found you, I found you," he continued, pulling Caleb back in again into another tight embrace that took some of his breath away.

His father dropped his head onto his son's shoulder and sobbed, rocking them both back and forth.

Caleb couldn't support himself, let alone his dad too, and he slowly fell over onto his back, bringing his father down with him. Carter clung to what was left of his son's shirt and continued to cry and cry, soaking the dirty, thin cloth through. Caleb was exhausted, but he managed to bring both arms up and embrace his father's heaving body as he continued to bawl out of pure joy.

"I'm alive," Caleb said barely audible, staring wide eyed up through the treetops, "I did it, I survived."

EPILOGUE

Caleb was rushed by his father that day back to the rental on the side of the highway and then on to the hotel where Carter and Layla had stayed during their search. At the hotel, the clerk was able to contact Emergency Services and an air ambulance was soon on its way. While waiting for the helicopter's arrival, Carter used the small first aid kit behind the front desk to clean Caleb's wounds as well as his own. The stab wound in Caleb's thigh was a mess and he flushed it with filtered water and then rubbing alcohol. His own wound, though deeper than he originally believed, didn't quite make it down to the muscle and would only require a few stitches in the end.

When the helicopter landed in the hotel parking lot and the paramedics came in with a stretcher, they immediately stuck a needle into Caleb's arm to get fluids and medicine into his system as quickly as possible. He wasn't dehydrated, thankfully, but the paramedics still did it as a 'just in case' step. They also gave him antibiotics to counter the infection, in addition to the clean bandage that Carter had just applied.

Caleb would not remember any of this later on when he awoke in the hospital. Neither would he remember the ride he and his father had taken in the helicopter, his first. Once he realized was rescued, he was able to let his guard down for the first time in over a week, and he just completely shut down. He slept for more than 48 hours straight after he was found.

When he finally awoke, he saw that he was in a hospital room with his mom and his sister, Amber. Apparently, his dad was also trying to catch up on some sleep on an oversized recliner in a room there at the hospital reserved for families of patients. Caleb was smothered with hugs and kisses from his mother and sister. Layla then ran out of the room to go and wake Carter. He was left with Amber for a few moments before the nurses rushed in to check on him and ask him some questions now that he was up. Caleb looked at Amber's teary, red face.

"Amber! I'm so happy to see you!" he burst out in a weak, scratchy voice that sounded like he was a character from a scary Halloween movie. This prompted more intense crying, tears of what he figured were tears of joy, and she crawled up onto the hospital bed and curled up next to Caleb, being careful to stay clear of his injured leg. Caleb wrapped her in his arms and said, "I'm so happy to see you. I love you." It felt so good to say that out loud to his sister, someone he had just days before resigned himself to never seeing again to share those words with.

The nurses came and went and Layla returned with Carter, who was now wearing a surgical-style scrub top and a pristine white gauze bandage on his upper arm. They were all now wedged together onto the bed with Caleb, a family once again. They stayed like that for a bit, then slowly removed themselves from the bed.

When Caleb had the mattress all to himself once again, he took full stock of the room he was in. There was all the typical beeping machinery and wires and tubes that one would expect, but the room was also bursting at the seams with cards, flowers, handmade posters, and stuffed animals. People were sending gifts to the hospital, as well as their home.

When the story broke that he was found after being alone in the forest for eight days, it became headline news all throughout the country and it also spread internationally. His survival tale was the inspiring, feel-good story of the year! Layla and Carter's phone numbers were apparently really easy to get because they had received dozens of calls and messages. Many coming from producers of popular morning television shows, afternoon and late night talk shows, as well as radio programs and book companies. There were even a few agents talking about how Layla and Carter should hire them to manage public relations and secure a movie deal! It was all so much.

Caleb's parents explained to him that, after he had been missing for a couple of days, a regional news outlet had picked up the story of his disappearance and began reporting on it. More interest was generated the longer he was missing. People had been contributing to a fund set up for his search which wound up, in the end, being enough to cover his parent's bills associated with the search—hotel, rental car, gas, etc. It was also sufficient to cover the gas that Dougie had used while searching the area in his plane.

There was more money left over in the fund and, after Caleb went home a couple days later, the family decided to give half of the money raised to the search and rescue organization for their assistance. All of the search and rescue team members were volunteers, but they still needed equipment to do their work. The money helped to maintain what they had and to purchase new items that they needed.

The other half of the money would be sent to the scouting organization Caleb was a part of, a big thank you for not only providing good role models to young, impressionable young men, but also for teaching their son the skills that in the end contributed to him surviving in the wild.

Before Caleb was cleared to go home, he had several guests. Most memorable to him was when Mr. Holman came by with the other scout leaders. The grown men could hardly keep their composure and cried freely, as they were both happy and upset at the same time. Happy, obviously, that he had been found and would make a full recovery from his ordeal. Upset, though, because they still bore the emotional weight of feeling like it was all their fault that they didn't keep better track of the boys, which resulted in him getting separated from the group.

"Mr. Holman, thank you for everything," Caleb beamed with a smile, "thank you for keeping me safe out there."

Holman had a look of mild confusion on his face. "I'm not sure why you're thanking me here."

"You spoke to me out there. You reminded me of all the things you and the other scout leaders have taught me and the others since joining the program. Mr. Holman, you helped me believe that I could do it."

At that, Holman wept anew, and with more force. Unable to contain himself, he reached forward, squeezed Caleb's hand with his, and exited the room with a quickness.

•••••

After Caleb was discharged, he did appear on

several shows and granted multiple interviews, but only one or two a day so he didn't get too tired, his body was still trying to heal after all. He was able to recount, with people he had only previously heard and seen on radio and television, his trials, his victories, and his failures. People couldn't get enough of "The Boy Who Survived". He was a minor celebrity for a while there.

Soon enough, life returned to normal. It wasn't long before school started up again. He was the most popular kid in school for the first week or so, everyone wanted to sit by him in class and be with him at recess. That faded quickly as kids went back to studying and hanging out with their own groups of friends, which was fine with Caleb. The attention was fun sometimes, but, more often than not, it was overwhelming.

Home life was back to normal too. He had chores to do and homework to complete. He still hadn't recovered enough to play sports, but that wasn't far off. He felt fine, but the delay in playing was more precautionary for now. His leg was the biggest reason playing sports was delayed. He walked normally, but if he tried to run his leg just felt weird and hurt if he was active for too long of a period or ran with too much intensity. He had, after all, inadvertently stabbed himself several inches into his leg muscles and then gotten an infection.

The last sign of life getting back to normal was that he sometimes got snotty with his parents over stupid things, like not putting dirty dishes in the dishwasher as he'd been told to do a thousand times. Caleb also argued regularly with Amber again—they were brother and sister after all—but never again was he ever mean to her or was he hurtful on purpose. They argued, but they forgave easily and did many things together that, before the incident, would not have happened. Sometimes they played games, other times they just hung out in each other's rooms. Caleb had survived his challenges and he would never again take his family, nor his life for that matter, for granted ever again.

ACKNOWLEDGEMENTS

A very big, heartfelt thank you to all the friends and family that helped me review and edit this, my first book. Thank you to all my scout leaders growing up, particularly B.O., that took us on many an adventure and somehow brought us home safely with only minor injuries...for the most part. Finally, thank you to my parents for instilling in me a love to read.

ABOUT THE AUTHOR

Benjamin Moore lives in Tucson, AZ with his wife, Luella, and three children: Elijah, Carli, and Sam. He is an Active Duty member of the United States Air Force and wrote this book while deployed to Ali Al Salem Air Base in Kuwait between flying combat missions in support of Operation Inherent Resolve.

Read more at benjaminmooreauthor.com

CPSIA information can be obtained
at www.ICGtesting.com
Printed in the USA
LVHW091929200621
690711LV00004B/30